DEADLY PROTECTOR

RED STONE SECURITY SERIES #19

KATIE REUS

Cover art: Jaycee of Sweet 'N Spicy Designs
Editor: Julia Ganis
Author website: https://www.katiereus.com

Deadly Protector/Katie Reus. -- 1st ed.
KR Press, LLC

ISBN 13: 9781635561951

For my mom, and all the other good moms, the world over.

CHAPTER ONE

"Think about what I said." Amelia LeBlanc patted Zamira's hand gently, the older woman's eyes kind as they stood near the TSA line.

Typical airport noise surrounded them, someone on the overhead speaker asking a couple to report to one of the gates, parents telling their children to hurry up. Zamira tuned most of it out and nodded at her former mother-in-law before she scooped her kids up against her for one more hug.

They'd just turned thirteen and were leaving with their grandparents for their annual spring getaway. Elisa, who normally groaned at any affection lately, hugged Zamira back tight. Andres did the same and there was a hint of wetness in his eyes. "I'm going to miss you both." She kissed both their faces, focusing on Andres until he finally laughed.

"We're going to miss you too." He adjusted his backpack and grinned, all hint of tears gone, which had been her hope with all the kisses. "And we'll talk every day."

"Yeah, Mom, this isn't the eighties," Elisa added with a hair toss. "We'll be able to FaceTime every day."

Zamira decided not to point out that she hadn't been born in the eighties. "I know, but I still get to miss my babies."

There was more grumbling, then her in-laws both hugged her and made promises to call or text each step of the trip so she'd know where her kids were and how they were doing. There was an innate gentleness in both of them. A kindness and caring that made it a lot easier to let her kids go with them.

She'd lucked out with her in-laws—just not with her long-deceased husband. She had no idea how her hotheaded husband had come from two such amazing people. The two lived on the outskirts of Kelowna in Canada, had a couple horses, and each year her twins spent time with them hiking, riding and all sorts of outdoor activities. Zamira normally went with them but the last couple years they'd gone alone and it had been good for all of them. She wanted her kids to experience the world, to gain a bit of independence, and to see how their father had grown up, to get a hint into who he'd been. Or who she'd thought he'd been. And she knew it was good for her to get some time to herself, to prepare for when or if they decided to move away for school. She hoped they didn't go too far.

"Oh, sorry," a man with a suitcase murmured as he jostled past her, his words and the movement jarring her out of her head. She needed to get out of here, to stop getting caught in a web from the past. Her life had changed the day her twins had been born—for the better.

And she was going to miss them. But like it or not she had two weeks to herself, so she was going to take advantage. Not be a sad sack.

As she left the airport, the automatic doors whooshed open and a humid breeze rolled over her—when an hour ago she'd needed a cardigan. Nothing like drunk Florida weather, unable to make up its mind. She slipped off her sweater as she made her way to the parking garage across from the terminal.

When she was about halfway under the concrete overhang, she

smiled to hear her sister Angel's familiar ringtone. Slipping her Bluetooth in, she said, "Hey. Checking up on me?"

"Nah. Just seeing if you're throwing a party tonight. If so, I'm bringing cupcakes."

"Ha ha." Zamira sidestepped a woman lugging a big suitcase behind her and picked up her pace. There was a lot of foot traffic and she wanted to get out of here—before she changed her mind and hauled her kids back home. Not that she was considering doing that. Not seriously. Mostly not. "They've been looking forward to this since last year."

"I can't believe you're letting them go for two weeks this time."

"I know, but it works with their school schedules and they're only missing a few days." The twins' school had a late spring break compared to some schools, in later April, and because the Friday before the break was a holiday, they were only missing three days total. "And I feel guilty because we're not taking our normal summer trip, so I agreed to two weeks. They're excited to get colder weather for a change."

"Hey, I'm not judging. I'm going to miss the munchkins but I'm glad you're getting some down time. I know Elisa has been giving you a lot of attitude lately."

She snorted as she hurried up the set of concrete stairs, bypassing the elevators and a dozen people waiting for the next ride. Being a single parent was not for the fainthearted. "She's eased up a little, surprisingly. I think Mama might have said something to her."

"I have such respect for Mama now, raising the four of us."

"No kidding." A horn blasted from somewhere on the second floor of the parking garage as she reached it and she winced. "Sorry about the noise. I'm almost to my car."

"No worries. So, you want to go out tonight? Or come over to our place?"

"Eh, maybe. I haven't decided if I'm looking forward to the quiet of the house or dreading it." She winced again as another horn blasted, but quickly slipped into her hybrid SUV and closed the door behind her. "I'll let you know. I'm kind of out of sorts right now. Also...Amelia said I needed to start thinking about dating again, that I shouldn't be afraid to see what's out there. She was pushing me in that gentle way of hers, but she was definitely pushing." She'd taken Zamira off guard.

"Man, I love that woman. You got so lucky with her. Thomas too. And she's right. You've been alone a long time. Not that there's anything wrong with it."

"I love my life," she said as she pulled out of the parking garage. "I'm so busy with my stuff and all the kids' stuff. I don't... even know when I'd have time." Or if she even wanted to find the time. Lucas had burned her. Not intentionally, and she hadn't realized who he'd been until he'd died, but knowing how blind she'd been to all his issues had shaken·her deeply. Shaken how she viewed men, relationships—her ability to make smart judgments.

"Hmm, smells like bullshit."

"You're annoying."

"Annoying when I'm right?"

"Ugh. Hey, hold on." She quickly paid the parking attendant, then rolled up her window as she pulled out onto the road. "And yes, super annoying."

"Clarita said something about one of your kitesurfing friends asking you out."

"Ah, not a friend really." She was part of an all-women's kitesurfing group that met once a week but lately there'd been a group of younger people meeting up at the same time near them. "The guy's just a rando who kitesurfs near my group and he's like, maybe twenty-three."

"So? You're only thirty-one."

"Thirty-two." She'd just had a birthday.

"Tomato, tomahto."

"A hookup isn't what I'm looking for." When her sister didn't respond, she cleared her throat. "That's what kids say now, right? Hookup?"

Angel snort-laughed. "I have no idea what 'the kids' are saying. And fine, you're not looking for a fling, so what are you looking for?"

"I don't know. The opposite of my past," she murmured.

"Oof." Angel was silent for a long moment. "What about that huge hottie from my wedding? The one you danced with a few times."

"Ah…" An image of Dimitri flashed in her brain. *Huge hottie* was an apt description of the man. And he certainly wasn't twenty-three. He was more likely forty-three and simply gorgeous. Big, broad shoulders, jet-black hair with just a bit of salt at the temples. His eyes were such a dark blue that they almost looked brown in darker settings. But in the light…

Gah, she had to stop thinking about him. It was hard though, considering she'd helped him during his physical therapy from a knee injury, had seen exactly how ripped he was all over. Well, she hadn't literally seen him *all* over, but his gym shorts and T-shirts couldn't hide his muscular physique.

"I was his physical therapist. So…" She'd met him at Angel and Juan's wedding—Juan knew him somehow, from work at Red Stone Security maybe—and the chemistry had been immediate, at least on her part. But he'd never asked her out, and then he'd ended up in her office needing physical therapy not long after. She'd thought he'd been into her, but he'd never made a move and they were just friends now. They were both so busy anyway. *Ugh.* This whole question was moot so she didn't even need to consider it.

"Oh my God, so what? You're not his physical therapist anymore. So you're legally allowed to date him if you want. You drive me crazy," Angel grumbled. "All my sisters drive me crazy. Mama is a saint. Just don't tell her I said that," she tacked on.

"I won't. And I think I'm going to say no for tonight. I'm going to head to the beach in a bit, get in some kitesurfing. It's a gorgeous day." She glanced out the window at the brilliant blue, cloudless sky. "I'll want to crash afterward and I doubt you want me to crash on your couch."

"You're always welcome, but I get it. Will you be at Mama's on Sunday?"

"Of course."

"Okay, see you then. Love you."

"Love you too." She opened her sunroof as she headed home, glad it was such a gorgeous day. Getting a healthy dose of salt water and sunshine was just what she needed.

YEP, this had been exactly what she needed, Zamira decided as she finished folding up her parachute. She would lay it out in the grass of her backyard later and blow off the stray sand with her pump, but she was ready to get home and relax. Her muscles were loose and she'd gotten a text from Amelia that everyone was now in Seattle and enjoying ice creams during the layover. Everything was good in her world.

"You gonna be out here next week?" Kia, one of her kitesurfing friends, a forty-five-year-old real estate agent, asked as she approached. In a low-cut one-piece blue bathing suit, she was stunning as always. She got out here more often than Zamira and it showed in every line of her muscular legs. "I know you've got some down time coming up."

"Definitely. I was thinking I'd be down here next Tuesday and Wednesday since there tends to be less traffic then." There were a lot of things she'd planned for her two weeks off, but she was definitely getting in extra kitesurfing.

"Ha, same. Good stuff then, I'll text you if anything changes but I'll plan on meeting up with you."

"Sounds good." Zamira stood, stretched as she looked out at

the ocean. The sky had shifted quickly, as it often did here. Gray clouds rolled in from the horizon and she'd been here for hours so it was a good time to leave. Before the thunder and lightning started.

"Zamira?"

She turned at the sound of a male voice, frowned slightly as a huge man approached her. In a white tank top and jogging-style pants that didn't quite fit his big frame, he didn't fit here either. No bathing suit, no towel or cooler. Something about him was familiar but she couldn't place him.

"Zamira LeBlanc?"

She blinked at the use of her former name. Lucas, her husband, had been gone a long time. She rarely thought of him anymore, had gone back to being Zamira Nowak.

Then it clicked into place where she knew this man from. *Ugh, great.* She feigned ignorance, however. "Ah, do I know you?" In her periphery, she was well aware of at least eight other kitesurfers close by and within shouting distance. Instinctively, she pulled the zipper on her rash guard top a little higher.

His jaw clenched as he approached, his eyes narrowing against the sun peeking out from the clouds. Or he was glaring at her, she wasn't sure.

Right about now, she was glad for her sunglasses. She started putting her kite into its bag and zipping it up as he reached her.

"I'm Kurt. I was friends with your husband."

She frowned as she picked up her backpack, slid it on. She wasn't going to bother getting dressed. Her bathing suit and rash guard had already dried and she wanted to get whatever this was over with and then get the heck out of here. "Oh, right... I thought you were, ah..." She trailed off, not wanting to call out that he'd been in prison.

His jaw clenched again. "I just got out of prison," he finally said.

The back of her neck prickled as he watched her, but she

raised her eyebrows, hoping she looked impatient and not scared. Because…why was he here? It was clear that it was to talk to her, not to go to the beach. So this wasn't a coincidence. Dread curled in her middle as that knowledge settled inside her. There was no reason for him to have searched her out. "Look, can I help you?"

"Why didn't you respond to my letters?"

"Letters?" She clutched the bag to her chest, her heart beating wildly. Years ago he'd sent some letters but she'd tossed them all. He'd gone to jail because of some scam or B and E thing, she wasn't sure. It had nothing to do with her or her husband. She'd heard he'd gotten out briefly, but had ended up getting tossed right back in after a violent bar fight or something. Maybe a robbery?

She hadn't thought of him in years—he was part of her husband's past and she didn't like to think about how stupid she'd been to marry Lucas. Didn't like to think about that part of her life at all. Not when she'd built something wonderful after him.

"Don't act like you didn't get them."

"Look, I have no idea—"

"Zamira, hey!" Zac, the annoying twenty-three-year-old who'd asked her out a couple times, jogged over in his board shorts, sporting a perfect tan. He was harmless and earnest and she was so grateful he'd chosen now to show up.

She smiled brightly. "Zac, hey!"

He looked a little shocked at her reception and his grin grew. Oh crap, she'd have to deal with his crush soon, but not at the moment.

Kurt looked as if he wanted to say more, but turned and stalked away through the sand. The band in her chest eased a fraction when he reached the long-planked walkway and headed toward the parking lot. But not totally. Because she didn't think this was over.

"I'm surprised you're here on a Friday." Zac's smile was easy, his expression open, and if she'd been the same age as him, she might have considered going out with him.

But she was the mom of teenagers and in a totally different phase of life. "My schedule opened up so I got some good water time." She glanced back at the horizon. "You might have to pack up early if that storm moves in." So far it was just gloomy out there but they both knew how quickly that could change.

"Yeah, probably... You want to grab a drink? We could head over to Coconuts." He chin-nodded at one of the beach places about a hundred yards down the strip, that was really just a hut with a bar. It catered to the college crowd with cheap beer and liquor. The little umbrellas in the coconut-shaped mugs didn't hide the fact that everything there was guaranteed to give you a headache the next morning.

"I'm done for the day, heading home. But ah, would you mind walking me to my car?" She glanced over at the walkway, didn't see Kurt anymore. But he could be waiting for her. She didn't understand why he was here but everything about his appearance unnerved her. He was a big guy who'd been in jail for a violent crime. She'd be crazy not to be cautious of his sudden appearance.

"Oh yeah, of course not. Was that guy hassling you?" He frowned, looking over at the parking lot.

"Kind of. And if you see him around, don't approach him. He's dangerous."

Zac straightened and she realized that had likely been the wrong thing to say. "Did he threaten you? You want me to call the cops?"

"No, no. I just meant that if you saw him loitering around, don't approach him or anything. He..." She shoved out a sigh, annoyed at herself for the mouth diarrhea. But now she needed to explain more. "Look, he was friends with my husband a long time ago. I have no idea why he showed up but he made me feel uneasy. And I know he was in prison for a while, so just steer clear of him if you see him hanging around here. Okay?"

"You're married?"

She bit back a sigh. That was his takeaway from what she'd said? "No. I was, a long time ago." Felt like a lifetime ago, and in some ways it was. She wasn't that same naive girl anymore.

"Couldn't have been that long ago." He eyed her with pure male interest then, his gaze sweeping over her bathing-suit-clad self from head to toe. Clearly it didn't matter that her long-sleeved rash guard covered everything.

And, okay, it was nice to have a hot guy check her out, but no. Just noooo. "I was eighteen and way too young to get married. I'm thirty-two now, Zac. And I know it's not a terribly huge age difference between us, but I'm not interested in dating right now. Okay?" He hadn't asked her out—this time. But he had before, and she knew where this was going.

He gave her that same affable grin she was certain had charmed many women out of their clothes and into his bed. "Yeah, no worries. Can't blame a guy for trying." He picked up her small cooler and board and fell in step with her as they headed to the walkway. "And I'll steer clear of the guy if I see him, promise."

"Thank you." She didn't see Kurt in the parking lot, but there were a lot of cars. He could be hiding in any one of them.

That knowledge set her on edge so she hurried as she packed up her things and left the parking lot. Normally after a day at the beach she was relaxed and rejuvenated. There was something about the scent of salt water—the feel of its traces still on her skin before she washed it off and lotioned up—that was soothing. She'd grown up spending most weekends on South Beach with her friends or sisters and now she took her kids often. It was part of her.

But now, she wanted to be anywhere but here. And...she couldn't help but wonder how he'd known she'd be here at all.

CHAPTER TWO

The same question kept replaying over in Zamira's mind as she pulled down her street. She'd taken an extra-long route home, and hadn't seen anyone who looked as if they'd been following her. But she still didn't feel better—because how had Kurt Ryba known she'd be at the beach?

She posted kitesurfing pictures on social media, but all her accounts were private. It seemed crazy that he'd followed her there, but...maybe it wasn't actually crazy. She couldn't understand why he'd want to talk to her though. He'd been friends with her deceased husband and she was pretty sure they'd probably been involved in criminal activities together.

As in, stealing cars.

Something she hadn't been aware of until right before Lucas had died. He'd been killed in a car accident that had been deemed just that, an accident. But...after learning the truth about him she'd always wondered if maybe there was more to it. Whether maybe someone he'd been involved with had killed him. She had no way of knowing, however. The cops had done an investigation and it had been listed as an accident. But it had never sat right with her.

She'd been so oblivious to that part of his life until one night he'd shown up at home covered in blood from a fight. He'd told her that he'd robbed the wrong guy with one of his "friends" and that she needed to go stay with her mom for a few days. So she'd taken the kids, who'd barely been one, and done just that.

Then...days later he'd been gone. She hadn't had time to process the fact that he'd been lying to her about who he was, much less process his death.

Even now, that part of her life seemed like a dream. Like, who had she even been back then?

Sighing, she pulled into her garage, but left the door open so she could unload her parachute. She still needed to do a thorough cleanout of the tubing on the kite to make sure no sand had built up. It took extra time, but she did it after every single session on the water. And it was why her parachute had lasted so long. As she was wrapping up, she heard her phone ringing from her backpack and nearly dove for it, thinking it was one of her kids.

But it was Dimitri.

She stared at the screen, her heart rate kicking up. They texted a couple times a week and occasionally met up for lunch if he was in the area near her work. She hadn't been his physical therapist for months so she was glad that she got to see him still. Even if she felt a little out of control when she was around him. Not in a wild way, just...she was so attracted to him and it scared her. She hadn't been with a man in a very long time and everything about Dimitri was intense.

So of course she answered. "Hey."

"Hey, yourself. How're you handling the kids being gone?"

She paused, pleased that he'd remembered. "It's only been a few hours, so relatively well. I spent the day out on the water which helped balance me out."

"Nice. Are you done for the day or did you want to grab dinner?"

"I'd love to." She jumped at the offer because if she was being honest with herself, she was scared to be alone. Not because her kids were gone, but because Kurt showing up at the beach today had rattled her. She still couldn't believe he'd just randomly known she'd be there.

Deep down she knew it wasn't random. He had to have followed her. Which meant he might know where she lived. It certainly wasn't a secret, likely wouldn't be hard to find out. She simply couldn't understand *why* he wanted to talk to her. She just knew she didn't want to be cornered by him again.

She realized Dimitri hadn't responded. "You still there?"

"Yeah, and great. I'll pick you up at six thirty if that works?"

"Perfect." It would give her enough time to shower and get ready. "I'll text you my address."

After they disconnected, she realized she had no idea what to wear. She hadn't been on a date in over a decade. Wait, was this even a date? Dinner felt different than casual lunch meetups. A wave of doubt swept through her. What the hell was she thinking?

"Get over yourself," she muttered to herself. This might not even be a date. He'd just asked her to dinner all casually. Friends did that, right? *Gah.* She'd figure it out later.

Either way, she was going to look amazing.

After hurriedly packing up her parachute and dumping her bathing suit and towel in the laundry room, she raced to her shower.

And couldn't fight the buzz of energy inside her. She had a date with *Dimitri.*

Probably.

After she'd showered and dried her hair, she called her sister Clarita using the video option.

Her sister thankfully picked up after a couple rings. "Hey, what's up? How are you doing?" Her expression was one of concern.

"I'm great," she said hurriedly. "And I have a date and he's going to be here in twenty minutes, and I have no clue what to wear."

Clarita's dark eyes widened and she actually squealed. Her older sister, who'd just turned thirty-three, sounded like a teenager. "Hey, don't judge! I'm allowed to be excited," she said when she saw Zamira's expression.

"I love you, but you've got to save the excitement for later and help me!" Panic had started to set in. This didn't feel like the casual lunch meetups from before and she wasn't sure why. "Maybe I should just cancel—"

"No. Okay, check Elisa's closet. There are four dresses in there, any of which will be perfect for you."

"What? Why?" she asked as she stepped out into the hallway and headed to her daughter's room.

"You can't be mad at me, but Elisa said that she thought you'd be going out on dates while they were gone and that you couldn't wear anything in your closet. She said…you'd end up looking like a beach bum. And then she had some other choice words about your clothing."

Zamira's mouth fell open even as she reached Elisa's closet. "Oh my God, she left me a note. What is wrong with that child?"

"What's it say?"

Zamira snorted as she read it. "It says 'Don't be mad at Tia C. She's just trying to help you. And you need her help. You need all the help, Mama.' I swear, that child." Sighing, she looked back at her sister, who was clearly fighting a laugh. "I don't know if I should be mad or not."

"No time for that. Grab the dresses, then head back to your room. You've got better lighting there. I suggest the emerald green one because you are glowing right now and it will look stunning on you."

"Then I'm trusting you." It had a bit more lace than she was used to but the dress was so pretty. And feminine. Her daughter was right—she'd have likely dressed in a beach dress or more likely beach-casual clothing because it was her comfort zone. But great things didn't come from comfort zones and she knew she needed to get out of hers. At least for tonight. Because even a couple months ago she'd have said no to a man asking her out to dinner. "Give me a minute," she said, setting her phone down as she quickly stripped off her robe and pulled the dress on.

It was sleeveless with a boat neck, and hugged her body perfectly, as if it had been made for her. It sort of flared right before her knees and wow, it really did look amazing.

"Let me see!" Clarita's voice called out.

Picking up the phone, she turned it so that Clarita could see her in the door mirror.

"It's perfect," Clarita sighed. "I wish I was there right now."

"This isn't prom." Though it felt more exciting than prom. And she hoped this night ended better than her own prom since her date had puked on her shoes.

"So what, you look amazing and I'm allowed to be excited. Wear medium-sized rose gold earrings, no bracelet because you'll fidget with it, and the dress doesn't need a necklace. Oh, and wear those cute sparkly sandals that wrap around your ankles. The ones with the faux-looking pearls and rose gold beads."

"The ones you gave me?"

"Yep." Clarita grinned. "And leave your hair down. Your curls are gorgeous. Oh my God, you're gorgeous. I hope you have fun tonight. Text me when you get home, I don't care how late. Unless you go to his place after," she said, wiggling her eyebrows. "And then text me in the morning with details."

Which just made Zamira laugh. "That won't be happening, trust me. But I'll text you regardless. And maybe don't tell Mama about this yet?" She wasn't ready to deal with questions or "suggestions" on men to date yet.

"I promise." Clarita glanced over at the sound of her husband Carlos's voice, then turned back to Zamira. "Carlos said he won't tell either. And he says to have fun."

"Thank you guys. I love you both." After she hung up and slipped on the sandals her sister had been right about—they were perfect—the doorbell rang.

Oh God, this was it. The first date she'd been on in over a decade. She could do this.

Hopefully.

CHAPTER THREE

Dimitri felt like what he imagined a nervous teenager would feel like when picking up a date. He'd never dated as a teenager. He'd been too busy stealing things, carving out a way to survive and then thrive.

Tonight…he was nervous. Zamira made him feel different in a way he couldn't quite define. She scared him, which probably meant he shouldn't be here.

But he liked her more than he'd ever liked anyone. The single mom was incredible and intimidating. And he'd been a Marine, had fought in Afghanistan—no one had ever scared him. But Zamira? Yeah, that was a different kind of fear. She was the kind of woman you held on to and he knew she was out of his league.

The door swung open and he nearly swallowed his tongue at the sight of her. Her deep green dress hugged her body in a way that had him imagining peeling it slowly from her, kissing every bronzed inch of her toned body. "You look beautiful," he murmured, holding out the small plant with a cluster of lilac buds he'd bought earlier in the day.

"Thank you. Ah, what is this?"

He cleared his throat, wondering if this had been a stupid idea.

Juan—who was fifteen years younger than Dimitri—had told him it was a great idea, so maybe...he shouldn't have listened. Then again, Juan had convinced Angel to marry him so clearly he got some things right.

"You said you'd been thinking of adding a couple more plants to your backyard and I thought this would be better than flowers." Because he remembered that she'd told him she was always sad when flowers died so she tended to buy plants for her house instead. He also remembered that she'd said she liked purple, which was why he'd bought the lilac plant. But he didn't want to come off as a complete weirdo so he left that out.

"This is so sweet! Come on in. I'll set this on the back patio and then we can leave."

"I'll carry it," he said when she went to take it. "I don't want you to get anything on your dress." It wasn't huge, just a sixteen-inch pot, but he didn't want to chance any soil getting on her.

Her cheeks flushed as she led him down a hallway and into the kitchen. "Thanks."

It was hard not to stare at her as she walked—she moved with a liquid grace that was mesmerizing. And her toned calves were incredible. And the fact that he was hot for her calves told him that he was more gone for her than he wanted to admit. But it was hard not to imagine them thrown over his shoulders as he tasted between her legs, gave her all the pleasure she deserved.

He'd have asked her out months ago at Juan's wedding, but he hadn't been certain of her interest. She was a difficult woman to read, which was probably part of the appeal. She was so confident and sure of herself. Then he'd hurt his knee and had been ordered to physical therapy—so he'd requested his doctor send him to her place for PT. Working with her had been heaven and hell because he hadn't been able to ask her out. But he had gotten to know her —and he liked *everything* he knew about her.

"Your house is very nice." An understatement. High ceilings, big open kitchen and living room that looked out onto a huge backyard and pool. He glanced around her backyard as they stepped out onto the patio and saw there was a volleyball area set up next to the small pool.

"Thanks. It's a lot quieter than it normally is with the kids gone."

"I bet. Have you heard from them?" It was clear that kids lived here, that there was energy and love in this big place.

"Elisa has sent me a couple Snapchat videos."

He blinked. "What's Snapchat?"

"A social media thing where you send videos that the viewer can see for a short time before they disappear. And I'm literally only on there for my kids and nieces and nephews, who are all on there. I like knowing what they're up to and I like that they want me to be part of their lives."

He simply nodded and set the plant near the edge of the lanai. "The woman I bought it from said it would need to be watered tomorrow evening and that it needs plenty of sun."

"Thanks. I'll take care of it and I appreciate the gift. It's really sweet."

His eyes fell to her mouth for a long, heated moment as he wondered if she would taste sweet, but he forced himself to not act like a caveman. "If you'd like, I can also plant it for you. I realize that giving you a gift that also requires you to work might not have been the smartest thing."

She let out a short, surprised laugh. "I didn't even think of it that way, and no, you don't need to plant it. I love to garden and I actually have the perfect spot for it."

"Okay, well, the offer stands if you change your mind. So who plays volleyball?" he asked as they headed back inside. Again, he had to force himself not to stare at her ass and legs. She was toned everywhere and it was impossible not to notice. She was one of the most active people he knew and it showed.

"Technically we all do, but Elisa plays for school and loves it. She's a lot better than I was at that age. She's also great at soccer, but her love for now is volleyball. And I hope she sticks with it once she gets to high school."

"That's gotta be soon, right?"

"Way too soon," she said as she grabbed a sweater by the front door, along with a small clutch.

The protective part of him was glad to see that she set her alarm when they left. And it was a good system too. He could break it, but most typical thieves wouldn't bother with this kind of system. He also noticed a few small cameras, but the lights didn't come on so he wasn't sure if they were active. He wanted to ask, to make sure she had them on, but knew he'd sound like a weirdo so he kept that to himself.

"It's really nice that you're letting them stay with your in-laws for a couple weeks."

"They're good people and love the kids. We were supposed to go up there in July but I've got too much on my plate with work, and the kids are both going to different sports camps over the summer. There's simply not enough time and…am I talking about my kids too much?"

He laughed lightly as he opened the passenger door of his SUV for her. "No. I want to know about you and your life, all of it. Not just the curated parts."

She shoved out a sigh, and for the first time since he'd met her he saw a spark of real lust when her gaze landed on his mouth. *Oh, hell yes.* He hadn't been certain before, but her look now was clear.

She definitely wanted him.

Well, the feeling was mutual.

Taking a chance, he half leaned over her and strapped her in. She smelled like the beach, a wild ocean scent that rolled over him. And when her gaze fell to his mouth again, he slowly leaned in and brushed his lips over hers, testing the waters. He'd been fantasizing about this since the moment he'd met her.

She made a soft moaning sound as she leaned into him, grabbing onto the front of his shirt. A shudder rolled through him—he hadn't been sure she would welcome this. As he tasted her, he forgot to think and breathe as her tongue flicked against his. He deepened the kiss, his body reacting immediately to the feel of her hands sliding up his chest, the taste of her...and he had to force himself to pull back before he lost his head fully. It was one of the hardest things he'd had to do.

Zamira blinked up at him as he looked down at her, her eyes dilated. "So this is definitely a date," she murmured.

Despite being rock-hard right now, he let out a laugh. "Definitely a date." He'd thought that was clear.

Her cheeks, which had flushed slightly, went even pinker. He forced more distance between them, had to make himself step back and shut the door. Because something told him if they kissed again, they might not make it to dinner.

That wasn't a bad thing at all, but he wanted to do things right with her. He didn't want casual with her. No, he'd done casual, usually preferred it, but with Zamira he wanted a lot more. He didn't want to simply jump into bed with her, and he hoped that wasn't all she wanted either.

Dimitri wanted to smack the little shit waiting on them—who couldn't keep his eyes off Zamira.

"Did you need a refill on anything?" The young man, who was maybe twenty, stared at Zamira as he asked.

"We're good," Dimitri said with more force than he'd intended. He'd never been rude to waitstaff but this guy was pushing his limits. "We'd just like some privacy," he added.

"Of course." The man hurried off, but not before giving Zamira puppy-dog eyes.

"If I was a betting man, I'd say he's going to give you his phone number by the end of the night."

She snickered as she took a sip of her white wine. "He's not very subtle, is he?" Then she looked around the restaurant again in a way that put him on edge. He knew she wasn't nervous around him, but she'd been looking around, as if searching for someone. On alert.

His protective instincts lit up. "Is everything okay?"

Nodding, she pulled her sweater off the back of her chair and slid it on. "Yes. I...okay, this is probably too much information for a first date, so..." She bit her bottom lip in a way that had his cock wanting to stand at attention. Everything she did seemed to have that effect.

"What is it?"

"It's probably nothing, but at the beach today this man showed up wanting to talk. Ah...he was friends with my husband, but I didn't really know him. He just got out of prison and he rattled me, demanding that I talk to him. He scared me, if I'm being honest. Sorry, I know this is probably a very odd thing to talk about on a first date. I just...thought I saw him earlier by the hostess stand when our waiter brought our drinks out. I was afraid he might have followed me from the beach earlier, but that's ridiculous. I'm just being paranoid. I shouldn't have said anything." She took another sip of wine, her hand trembling slightly.

Anger spiked through him at some asshole harassing her. She didn't strike him as a paranoid person, but he decided not to push. Too much. He needed to know she was safe. "Is that why you agreed to go out with me? You were afraid to stay home tonight?" That...was a hit to his ego. But if she was in danger, he wanted to keep her safe.

"No," she said quickly. "I mean...I definitely wanted to go out with you. But you called at the right time, if I'm being honest. Oh my God, I'm mucking this all up. I'm so happy to be here tonight."

He reached across the table, took one of her hands in his. "And I'm happy you're here too. If you're worried about anything, I can have someone run this guy's info, dig into him a bit." He'd do it himself if he could convince her to give him the guy's name.

"No, it's fine. Let's talk about something else. Anything else. Juan mentioned you've been picking up more contract jobs with Red Stone. How's that working out?"

If Juan had mentioned him, maybe she'd been asking about him? Dimitri could hope. "It's challenging and I enjoy it. I still keep tabs on my stores, but I have good managers in place at all of them. It allows me to take on more contracts for Red Stone." He'd been surprised when they'd first reached out to him.

Red Stone Security had a reputation for being "Boy Scouts" as his friend Viktor liked to say. And Dimitri definitely was not one. He'd only been caught breaking into a place once, when he'd been eighteen, but the owners of Red Stone weren't stupid. And they employed some of the best hackers in the country—they would know he'd worked on the wrong side of the law for a very long time. Now he was a successful owner of hardware stores all across Miami and Homestead.

"Can I ask how you got tapped by them, I guess is the right phrase? Because Juan made it very clear that it's difficult to get hired to do contract work for them. Or difficult to get hired by them at all—he's a big fan of yours, by the way."

Okay so he was definitely buying Juan a drink next time he saw him. Or paying the guy back somehow. Dimitri lifted a shoulder. "Ah, they started a new division a few years ago and the woman who runs it thinks outside the box. She reached out to me because we had mutual contacts and wanted to know if I'd like to try something new."

"So, you're paid by companies to break in and steal from them? How exactly does that work? It seems really different from running a bunch of hardware stores." She paused as their waiter delivered their salads.

Thankfully the guy didn't loiter this time, just gave her that same puppy-dog look and left.

"It is different. Luckily my stores are all run by capable managers." He'd started his first hardware store when he'd decided to go legit, and things had snowballed from there. "As far as the work I do for Red Stone, I can't give too many details, but we work as a team, targeting various weaknesses. It shows companies where they can shore up security issues." Which, in this ever-changing world, was a smart thing to do. "They're almost always surprised, but grateful."

"That's really cool." She took a sip of her wine and smiled at him, her expression open and sweet, and God, he was still surprised she'd gone out with him.

He'd never dated a single mom before, had pretty much stuck to casual sex for as long as he could remember. But Zamira made him envision a different kind of life. One he was afraid to admit he wanted. His life was very orderly and he'd always been fine with that. But he wanted more. He cleared his throat. "Well, I'm a big fan of your job."

She laughed lightly. "How are you feeling anyway? You seem to have no lasting effects."

"I'm walking fine now. Jogging too." He still wanted to kick his own ass for his stupidity.

"Climb any big ladders lately?"

"Ha ha, no." He'd hurt himself by not properly stabilizing a ladder at one of his stores before he'd climbed on it. It was his own damn fault he'd gotten hurt and he knew it could have been a whole lot worse.

"I'm glad you're doing well."

"Me too." His gaze fell to her mouth, but didn't linger. He didn't want to get caught up in thoughts of kissing her. That way lay distraction. "So what are your plans for the next couple weeks?"

"I took off work and I plan to do some boring house stuff, but I'm also planning to get a lot of uninterrupted time out on the water. And I'm pretty sure Mila wants to have a girls' day at her and Lyosha's place. So I'm definitely going."

He grinned as he speared a piece of lettuce. "I don't blame you." He'd been friends with Lyosha for over a decade, and the man had a house in one of the most expensive neighborhoods in Miami. Now he was married to Mila, Zamira's younger sister.

"Oh, I've also been invited out on a friend's boat for a deep-sea fishing trip. I don't actually fish, but I love the idea of being on the water all day."

Dimitri wondered if this friend was male, but shelved the thought. Mostly. Because he was very curious. "I hope to be able to take you out over the next couple weeks. More than once." *How about every day?*

"I'd love that." Her cheeks flushed slightly and she barely glanced at their waiter as he picked up their salad plates.

The most primitive part of Dimitri was glad. He wanted her eyes only on him.

Through the rest of dinner Zamira was relaxed, and he hated when it finally came time to leave. It was too soon for him to invite her to his place. Not for him, but too soon for her, he was certain. "When can I take you out again?" he asked, leaning back in his chair after paying. "It doesn't have to be dinner. There are a couple art shows in the coming weeks we could go to. Or maybe you can teach me to kitesurf."

Her eyebrows raised slightly. "Really?"

"Yeah, it looks fun." Lies. It looked like something twenty-year-olds did, but he would get out there and try it, if it meant spending time with her.

"I've got enough extra gear that you could borrow...but no pressure. Kitesurfing isn't for everyone. We can go kayaking instead or try one of those glow kayaking things."

"Glow?"

"There are a couple rental places that offer nighttime kayaking or paddleboarding. The boats all glow and light up the area underneath and around you. It looks fun but neither of my kids has wanted to try it."

"I'm in."

"Great. How about Sunday night, then? I can't tomorrow."

His instinct was to ask why she couldn't tomorrow but that was most definitely not his business. He'd never been a jealous man, but with Zamira... Yeah, he needed to lock down whatever those feelings were. She wasn't his, even if he wanted her to be. And acting like a caveman wouldn't win him any points. "Works for me."

"Okay, well I'm paying for kayaking since I'm inviting you."

He gave a soft snort as the waiter returned. He didn't care if he was old-school, he wasn't comfortable with a woman paying for a date.

"What does that sound mean?" she asked as he set the bill back on the table after giving a big tip. The guy might have been checking out Zamira, but he'd been good at his job.

"It means we'll see."

She let out a surprised laugh. "That's what I tell my kids when the answer is no. You're very sneaky."

He just grinned and placed his hand on the small of her back as he led her out of the restaurant and into the waiting area. The place was large, with a plush bar that had filled up a while ago as people without reservations decided to brave trying to get a table. When Zamira stumbled, he slid his arm around her shoulders, but paused when he saw how pale her face had gotten.

He tensed. "What's wrong?"

"The man I told you about, from the beach. He's here. By the bar."

Oh hell no. This guy was not messing with her. "Don't look at him, okay?" He cupped her cheek, so she'd look only at him. "What's he wearing?"

"Ah..." She blinked once. "Black button-down was all I could see. He's a white guy, ah, he's tall, has a buzz cut, and he's standing next to a woman in a cobalt blue dress. They're not together, or I don't think they are. He's turned away from the bar, his back against it, and he was staring at me as we entered the bar."

Dimitri nodded and slipped his phone out covertly. "I'm going to get a picture of him, okay?"

She looked confused, but nodded.

"Lean in and smile," he murmured, holding the phone up in front of them. He'd never taken a selfie before. As soon as he'd snapped a picture of the two of them, he quickly switched his phone onto video mode, then turned with his phone, casually scanning the bar before he tucked it away.

Got you, he thought.

"Why did we do that?"

He slid his arm around her shoulders again. "One, because I wanted a picture of you, and two, I didn't think you'd give me his name. Now I'm going to find out exactly who he is no matter what."

She stared up at him looking a bit shocked as they headed out of the restaurant. "You really are sneaky."

He shrugged, not apologetic at all. "It's not a coincidence that he's here. And since he is, he followed us somehow. It's possible he followed us from your house, but I didn't see anyone tailing us."

"Were you watching?"

He paused, thought about it as they stepped outside into the cool night air. Normally he paid attention to everything. "I was distracted tonight," he finally murmured. And he hadn't known there was any cause for concern. So it was very possible someone had followed them, especially given Miami traffic.

"His name's Kurt Ryba," she finally said as they headed across the street.

Dimitri occasionally used valet, but as a former thief, he didn't like giving his keys or property into the care of anyone he didn't know. He frowned at the name. It was...familiar, but he couldn't place why. As they reached the other side of the street he glanced behind them, and Ryba was standing by the valet watching them.

Dimitri's hackles rose but he fought off that primitive instinct to approach the man now. That would be stupid and he was a patient man. "Don't turn around, but he's watching us."

Zamira shivered, but didn't turn. "I'm sorry about all this."

Frowning, he glanced down at her as they entered the four-story parking garage. "Why are you sorry?"

"This whole deal, whatever it is." Her expression was pinched and he wasn't having it.

"None of this is your fault." Luckily he'd gotten a spot on the first level, so as soon as he'd opened the passenger door for her then gotten in himself, he sent off the video to Lyosha along with the man's name. Later, Dimitri would look into Ryba himself, but he wanted Lyosha to jump on it if possible. He wanted to keep Zamira safe, to protect her—to resolve whatever this was for her.

As he started the engine, a text pinged from Lyosha.

Why the hell are you out with my sister-in-law?

Dimitri's eyebrows raised at the protective tone. But maybe he shouldn't be surprised. Lyosha was fiercely protective of his wife and he'd basically adopted all of Mila's family—or more like he'd been adopted by them. And it was clear his longtime friend, who'd never had a family until now, would do anything for them.

Just look into it. The guy followed us to a restaurant and has been hassling her. I need to know the danger level.

"Do you mind if I take this?" Zamira asked as her phone started ringing. "It's my kids. They want to do a video chat."

"Of course, go ahead." He'd wanted to dig more, to get more details about this Ryba asshole, but it could wait.

"Mija, mijo!" Her whole expression brightened as she held the phone up to look at her kids.

"Mama!"

Both kids started talking, one over the other, telling her about their day, their travels, how long it had taken to drive up to

Kelowna, how they would be riding horses as soon as they woke up.

Then... "Where are you?" Elisa asked.

"Oh...ah." Zamira shot him an odd look, then looked back at the screen. "I'm just out with a friend."

There was a pause, then, "You're wearing one of the dresses from Tia C! Oooh...okay, we love you and we'll talk to you later!"

"Wait, I'm not done telling Mama—" Andres started, but the call ended.

Zamira let out a sigh, then tucked her phone away.

"What is it?"

"Nothing. Elisa knows I'm on a date. It's why she hung up."

"Is that a bad thing?" He was new to this whole "dating a single parent" thing.

"No, not really. I've just..." She gave him a weird look again.

"What?"

"It's embarrassing, but I haven't really dated since Lucas died. I've never brought anyone around my kids, ever. I just...I don't know, I thought Elisa would be weird about it, but she seems almost happy. Which is great. Just surprising."

He didn't know what to say to any of that. He knew she was a widow, but didn't know all the details of her life. He cleared his throat. "So tell me what you know about this Kurt Ryba and his relationship to your husband."

"You sure you want to hear all this? It's a lot for a first date. And I might be out of practice, but even I know this isn't first date talk."

"We danced a few times at Juan and Angel's wedding, so this could be considered a second date. And this is appropriate second date conversation." He kept his tone light, which made her laugh.

"That was not a date, but I appreciate it. Okay, fine... Right before my husband died, I found out that he wasn't who I thought he'd been. The twins were barely a year old, and after they'd been born things had started to fracture between us. Not...big stuff, at first, but I started seeing red flags that I should have seen before we got married and I got pregnant. But I was eighteen when I fell for him and we got married fast. He was my first everything and I fell hard. Probably had actual stars in my eyes." She rolled her eyes at herself.

"Don't be hard on yourself. When I was eighteen, I got arrested for breaking into a celebrity's house on Star Island."

She blinked, her gorgeous mouth falling slightly open. "Seriously?"

"Yep. So whatever you're going to tell me, I promise I'm not judging."

"Okay, well, we're going to go back to that later because I want details."

A grin tugged at his mouth. "That's not a problem."

She nodded, then took a breath. "Anyway, he came home one night and things just suddenly shifted. He'd been in a big fight apparently and was worried for our safety so I packed up the kids and headed to my mom's. We talked some over the next couple days and he said he was 'fixing things' and then he died. Just like that. It was a car accident, but I never really knew for sure." She looked at him, her dark eyes wide. "And I never wanted to know if it was more. I was scared of the answer, scared of the kids knowing their father was a criminal. I was able to figure out that he stole cars and sold them either for parts or just changed the VINs and resold them as different vehicles. And Kurt, he was friends with my husband. Or I assume they were. I swear I don't know their connection, but I do remember him from the funeral. He attempted to talk to me, but I don't remember much about that day. I was still in a state of shock. Then he got sent to prison almost immediately after, and I only know that because he mailed me a couple letters."

Dimitri shot her a surprised look as he pulled up to a stoplight. "What did they say?"

"No idea. I tossed them. I didn't want anything to do with

Lucas's former life. I was still reeling, trying to keep it together. Then after I moved with the kids into a bigger house, I never heard from him again. I figured whatever it was he wanted, it wasn't important. And I haven't thought of him in over a decade."

Dimitri digested everything, and as his cell phone buzzed with an incoming text he pulled up to another stoplight. He quickly read the message and froze at Lyosha's text.

"Change of plans. We're headed to my place."

CHAPTER FOUR

"So...what's the deal?" Zamira asked as Dimitri ushered her into his house. He lived in a large house right on the water, and his driveway had a gated entrance. Nothing was completely secure, but she felt as if they'd be safe here. And clearly he thought that was what she needed. He'd been cautious driving here, taking a long way to make sure they weren't followed.

"Lyosha sent me some information on Kurt Ryba," he said as they stepped into his kitchen.

Everything was clean—no, pristine. All high-end appliances and lots of grays and earth tones. Not much color or mess anywhere. Not like her kitchen which, sure, wasn't messy, but it was definitely used.

Her kids left their homework on the island top and usually hung their backpacks off their stools at the island instead of in the mudroom where they had hooks. And she had two bowls on the island always filled with snacks for the kids—one with fruit and the other with treats. Her refrigerator was covered in pictures of the kids, her familia and her ever-changing calendar. His fridge had one magnet on it—for a takeout place.

She knew they were different, but this highlighted it in a way that made her shift uncomfortably. She wasn't sure she was ready to start dating again, especially someone who had a very different lifestyle than hers.

"Sit, please." He motioned to the big island with a granite countertop. Then he grabbed a bottle of red wine from a well-stocked rack and held it out.

She nodded, figuring she'd need it.

"He looked familiar but I couldn't figure out why until Lyosha got back to me." He popped the cork and pulled down a glass.

"Is he going to be discreet about whatever this is?" She loved her family, but they could be a lot sometimes, and if they found out about this, they would bombard her.

Dimitri lifted a shoulder. "He'll probably tell Mila."

Mila might keep all this to herself, at least for a bit. Zamira nodded for him to continue.

"Do you know who Irene Gorcyca is?"

"Ah…she owns a real estate company, right? I think I've seen her billboards." A pretty older woman with sharp cheekbones and a white smile.

Dimitri snorted softly. "She does own a real estate company. She also runs designer drugs along the East Coast, owns probably three dozen strip clubs from here to Orlando where she most definitely launders money. She also pulls a few heists a year. She's smart and keeps her criminal enterprises diversified, I'll give her that. She's never been arrested, but it's known among certain circles that if you cross her, you'll end up dead. Or never seen again and assumed dead," he corrected.

Zamira's stomach twisted. "What does that have to do with Kurt?"

"She's his aunt. And I've met him before, but it was a long time ago. It was why I recognized him. He was thinner then. Younger." He slid a glass to her, his expression grim. "Clearly he bulked up in prison. Lyosha's digging more into his time inside and I'm going to be reaching out to my own contacts. But if Ryba

33

wants to talk to you, it's not good. And you need to get ahead of it."

"What does that mean?"

"It means that I'm going to talk to him for you."

"Dimitri—"

"No. It's not up for discussion. I'm doing it. But I need to understand more about why he's contacting you."

"I told you, I have no idea."

His expression was unreadable as he watched her, but then he sighed. "He used to be part of a violent carjacking crew."

Zamira sucked in a breath. "Was Lucas…part of that?"

"No. From what Lyosha's found out, Lucas was small-time. But there had been some contact between him and Ryba in the weeks before your husband died and before Ryba got put away."

"Contact?"

"Phone calls. And records of texts."

"Lyosha found all that?"

Dimitri nodded.

That was a little scary. She'd known that her new brother-in-law did well for himself, but she hadn't realized he was a hacker. "Okay, so what does this mean?"

"That they were definitely linked. We just don't know how. Yet. They could have done a job together or been planning to do a job. Or maybe Ryba gave something to your husband and thinks you still have it. Whatever it is, we need to figure out what, and fast. Because if his aunt is involved in whatever this is, she has a tendency to strike hard first and ask questions later."

Zamira shuddered, wrapping her arms around herself. She was so glad her children were out of the country. Still… "My kids?"

He shook his head. "Not in any danger. You might want to let your in-laws know to be on the lookout for anything out of the ordinary but…sending someone after kids across country borders is very, very risky and expensive. And Ryba has no money."

"What about his aunt?"

"So far Lyosha doesn't think she's involved. Ryba's phone records since getting out show that he's had exactly one phone conversation with her. One she initiated, likely to tell him to keep his nose clean."

"Okay so…what's the plan? What do I need to do?"

"For now, nothing. I'm going to reach out to Ryba and set up a meeting."

She slid off her seat and rounded the island, shaking her head. "I can't ask that of you."

"You're not asking. I'm offering."

"Okay fine, I can't let you."

He gave her a look that was pure male power as he shook his head. "I'm doing it."

She stared up at him, a mix of emotions warring inside her. It was a relief to have someone helping her, but at the same time, they weren't in a relationship. Not really. "You can't just take over like this."

He slid one of his big hands onto her hip, clutched her in what she could only describe as a possessive grip. "I am. Your safety matters to me. And…I used to be a different person than I am now. I wasn't into violence like Ryba, but I still lived on the other side of the law."

Given what he'd said about being caught breaking into someone's home, that wasn't a complete surprise. She stepped an inch closer, placed her hands on his chest, felt the steady beat of his heart. And couldn't help but notice how incredibly muscular he was. Damn. *No, focus.* "And that means you're the one who meets with him?"

"It means I speak the same language as him. We know some of the same people so he knows I'm not involved with law enforcement. If you go to meet him, he'll strong-arm you. If I meet him, I might be able to get answers. Or at least figure out what he's angling for. Did your husband have any bank accounts or a storage unit separate from your household stuff?"

"No. Not that I know of anyway. I went through everything pretty thoroughly after..." She cleared her throat. "My mama helped me too. I've got some of his stuff packed away. Some I gave to his parents and some I saved for the kids. But nothing worth anything really."

He was quiet for a long moment, then said, "I think you should stay here tonight. In one of my guest rooms," he added quickly when she tensed. "I'm going to reach out to Ryba and I want you where I know you're safe when I meet him."

"Dimitri, this is too much. I can't—"

He grasped her hip again, squeezing as he tugged her to him. As he did, he shifted ever so slightly so that he pressed her up against the island, pinning her in place with his body. Despite everything, heat spiraled through her at the feel of his powerful frame against her.

"You're not asking me to do this. I'm insisting. Do you really want to meet with Ryba alone? You've got two kids to think about and he's an ex-con with an unknown agenda."

She hated that he was right. And she hated that he might be putting himself in danger for her. "You'll meet somewhere public?"

"Of course." He wrapped his arms around her, pulling her close.

She did the same, sliding her arms around his back as she laid her head on his chest. This all felt surreal. She might hate that he was being pulled into this mess, but she was glad to have him on her side. He made her feel safe—and that worried her. She'd made a mistake with trusting her husband and she could be making one right now. "What kind of gray-area things did you use to do?" she murmured.

He chuckled slightly, the sound reverberating through her. And when he pulled back and looked down at her, raw heat flared in his dark blue eyes. A thrill of warmth rolled through her. Then he gave a soft groan and stepped back. "I need to make some calls."

A sense of loss swamped her as he moved away. She wanted to pull him to her, to wrap herself around him. "So you're not going to answer my question?"

"I will, just not tonight. I need to reach out to some people, then make contact with Ryba. And the sooner the better. I want to get that taken care of. First I need a better picture of who he is."

Of course. She just hated all of this. "Thank you for doing this. For helping me." She wasn't sure what she would have done. She wasn't even sure she would have thought to go to Lyosha. He loved her sister, there was no doubt of that. But he was still fairly new to their lives. She might have called Juan, since he worked for Red Stone Security and she'd known him for a long time. He had a lot of contacts. But Dimitri was taking over so smoothly and... she was letting him.

Because she was afraid. For herself, her kids. Her family. And her kids only had her left. It was a knowledge she was very aware of at all times. It lived in the back of her brain, an extra worry that simply existed inside her. Sure, they had her family. And if something happened to her, she knew her sisters and mama would step up. But they'd already lost one parent. She didn't want them to lose both. And she didn't want to miss out on seeing them grow up because she'd taken a stupid risk.

"I'll do anything I can to help. And for the record, whatever happens between us—or doesn't happen between us—I'm helping you. I don't want you to feel pressured for...anything." He cleared his throat, looking uncomfortable.

Which just made her smile. "I don't feel pressured." Just hot for him, and she wondered if there was something wrong with her. She was definitely worried and on edge, but...she was also very aware of Dimitri as a man. And very aware that it had been a long time since she'd been with one. Something about Dimitri made her want to throw caution to the wind—along with all of her clothes.

"Good." He shoved out a sigh, then straightened. "I'm probably going to have to bring Juan into this. He needs to know because I want someone to keep an eye on your house. I saw cameras at your house. Are they hooked up?"

She nodded. "Yeah, a few. They're all set on motion sensor and I get everything streamed to my phone."

"Good. That's covered, then. I don't have any clothes that will fit you, but for tonight at least you can sleep in one of my shirts."

Or in nothing at all.

The words were on the tip of her tongue but she held them back. He wanted to take care of this mess and she wanted him to as well. Even so, disappointment punched through her that this was how their date was ending. After he'd kissed her, far too briefly in the vehicle earlier, she wanted more. "That's great, thanks."

He nodded and pulled his phone out, responding to a text even as he started to show her where the guest room was.

Zamira saw Lyosha's name and wanted to ask questions, but Dimitri seemed too intense right now and he was doing her this huge favor.

As fear and need battled with each other inside her, she simply thanked him for the extra clothing and for keeping her safe tonight.

CHAPTER FIVE

Zamira shot up in bed, her heart kicking against her chest. It took only a second for her to settle, for the remnants of her dream to fade. A bear had been chasing her through the woods, its claws flashing under the bright moonlight.

She was safe. So were her kids. "Stupid dream," she muttered, shoving the covers back. She'd finally fallen into a fitful sleep about...four hours ago, she realized when she saw the clock on the guest room nightstand. It was only three in the morning. Way too early to be up.

Before she'd gone to bed, Dimitri had checked on her a few times, but it had been clear he'd been distracted so she'd assured him she was fine. She'd tried to watch a little television, then she'd found his library and picked a couple books. But nothing had been able to hold her attention so she'd finally managed to doze.

Clearly too much had been on her mind because she'd had a dream about an attacking bear. What even was that? So weird. Or maybe it was just tied into Ryba harassing her.

She lay back down, listening to the quiet of Dimitri's house. His place was huge; she hadn't even seen most of it. Just the kitchen and living room, which were connected, and the hallway that led to the guest bedroom she was in. Which was gorgeous but a bit cold, decor wise. Similar to the kitchen, it was grays and earth tones with oversized paintings showing the downtown Miami skyline at different times of the day and year. The bathroom was huge with an oversized tub and everything was so white and sparkly. It was like she was staying in a fancy hotel.

After a few minutes she realized she wouldn't be able to go back to sleep so she got out of bed and made her way to the kitchen. It was dark under Dimitri's closed door as she passed by. Not that she'd expected him to be up.

She could at least get some coffee and maybe use his pool before he got up. He'd said his place was secure, and given the gated entryway and the private pool and patio area, she believed him.

Since she didn't want to wake Dimitri, she was extra quiet in his kitchen—and his coffeemaker barely made any noise. After two cups of coffee and the house was still noiseless, she knew she'd go crazy if she couldn't burn off some of her energy and, okay, anxiety. She'd already checked her cell and could see on her family's linked app that her kids were of course at their grandparents' and very likely sleeping given that they were three hours behind her. And their phones were in sleep mode—she'd checked.

She knew they were safe, she just hated not being able to see them and hug them after the surprise visits—aka pseudo stalking —by Kurt Ryba. Better they were in Canada than here, however.

Decision made, she grabbed a towel and robe and slipped out onto the back patio area. It was already lit up with what she guessed were solar lights. The pool and yard beyond were walled in and gorgeous palm trees skirted most of the property.

After braiding her hair, she slipped off her robe and slid into the pool, savoring the feel of the warm water enveloping her as she waded deeper. Her mama had called her a water baby from the time she was four. And it was true. Thankfully her kids loved all forms of water as much as she did so they got a lot of time outdoors.

Diving underwater, she tried to shelve all her churning thoughts, to find a way to de-stress through laps. She didn't bother counting her laps, just kicked and stroked, back and forth, back and forth until her legs and arms started to feel the burn.

As she came up for air and started to shove off the wall at the deep end for another lap, a light in her periphery flipped on.

She stopped and turned toward the house—and realized that Dimitri was sitting on the edge of one of the lounge chairs. "Hey, did I wake you?" The sun wasn't up yet, but the edge of the sky had started to brighten, promising a no doubt beautiful sunrise soon.

His mouth curved up in the sexiest way as he stood and strode toward her. "I was working out in my gym when I got an alert that the patio door was opened. You're a strong swimmer."

Zamira stayed where she was, propping her arms up on the edge of the pool and keeping her breasts out of view because she was very aware that she was just wearing her panties. She was comfortable in her skin, and occasionally hit up nude beaches along the coast, but this felt different. "Is it okay that I'm out here? I figured it was safe and I needed to burn off the energy." She hadn't been diagnosed with ADHD until she was seventeen, and so many things had clicked into place then—and she'd discovered that staying active helped keep her focused in other facets of her life.

"It's definitely fine. Full disclosure, I've got cameras out here," he said as he crouched down close to her.

"Oh…" Was he trying to tell her that she was on camera while swimming mostly naked?

"They're not recording you. They're mostly facing toward the wall and perimeter areas, but once I got the alert you were out here, I turned off the one that faces the pool."

She grinned. "Thanks."

"Are you hungry or did you want to get in some more laps?"

"I could definitely eat."

He nodded and stood, backing up and giving her space. "You want me to bring you your robe and towel?"

"Sure, thanks."

He grabbed her things and set them by the edge of the pool, careful to keep his gaze above the water. "I'll be in the kitchen when you're ready." Before he turned away, his gaze landed on her mouth and raw lust flared there for a moment.

Heat spiraled through her and she watched as he walked back inside, admiring his long strides and sculpted ass. His gym shorts were loose, but his ass filled them out perfectly—it filled out every single thing he wore perfectly.

Part of the reason he'd recovered so quickly from his knee injury was because he'd already been in great shape. And she wondered...well, she wondered a lot of things. Like if he'd have stamina in bed. Oh, she imagined he would, but she couldn't sit out here and drool over him so she hurried out of the pool.

After wringing most of the water out of her hair and drying off, she wrapped up in the robe and slid her panties off, tucking them away in her wet towel. She'd worry about drying them later.

Inside, she found Dimitri at the stove with a carton of eggs, diced vegetables and cheese on the countertop next to him. "You do use this kitchen." It was so clean, she hadn't been sure. She grinned as she took a seat on one of the stools across from him.

That full mouth of his curved up again and she felt that wicked grin like a punch to all her senses. "Occasionally. I'm very self-sufficient, though I do prefer takeout."

"I like a self-sufficient man."

His gaze strayed to her mouth again and yeah, that lust was just simmering under the surface now. He wasn't hiding it at all and she found that incredibly hot. Then he tucked it away as he nodded at the eggs. "Is scrambled eggs okay?"

"Perfect. I'm normally not a big breakfast person, but after all those laps I'm hungry. Did you want help?"

"Nah, just relax. I've got this. Did you want more coffee?"

"Actually, yeah. I could go for another cup." She slid off the stool and made another cup. "Want me to top you off?"

He nodded as he cracked another egg into the bowl. "I've got to run out for an hour, to talk with someone about Ryba," he said after she slid back onto the stool.

Shivering, she wrapped her fingers around the mug. "Is that good news?"

"Yeah. Just need to go over some things," he said vaguely. "And I've also got Ryba's contact information. I'll be reaching out to him this morning after my meeting."

She wanted to tell him that he didn't have to, but he'd jumped feetfirst into this thing and she found that she trusted him. He seemed to have a much better handle on this situation and she could admit she needed the help. "Thank you. I know you said you'll be meeting with him, but if you think I should be there—"

He shook his head, shot her a sharp look. "No way."

She held up her palms. "I was just offering in case things had changed."

"They haven't. How'd you sleep?" He poured the whipped eggs into a pan already sizzling with butter as he asked.

"Not great, but that had nothing to do with your guest bed, which was very soft. What I've seen of your place is fantastic. And you have a gym too?"

"A small one. And my bed is very soft too, for the record."

She blinked, surprised at his bold words.

He glanced over his shoulder, still manning the stove as he grinned. "Just thought I'd throw that out there."

Her cheeks warmed as she said, "Noted." She cleared her throat, feeling out of sorts, but in a good way. She was way out of her comfort zone right now—she hadn't stayed at a man's place since her husband. This was new territory, and despite the crap show going on in her life she found she liked being at Dimitri's place. Even if she was a bit nervous at the thought of having sex again. "I'd like to grab some of my things if I'm going to be staying here for another day or so?" They hadn't really discussed beyond today. "Or I can go to my mom's or—"

"Here is fine. Better than fine," he tacked on as he added cheese to the mix. "I like you here. And I already talked to Juan last night. He's going to be here in an hour while I meet with my friend. He'll take you to your place so you can grab whatever you need. Pack for a week or two."

"That's…a lot." Not to mention, now Juan knew what was going on. Which meant she'd need to talk to her family about all this very soon.

He lifted a broad shoulder. "Better safe than sorry. It's good your family knows about this anyway," he added, as if he'd read her mind.

She took a sip of her coffee. "So who are you going to meet with?"

"Someone who knows Ryba's aunt. Well, knows her better than I do. I want to get a feel for what we're up against."

The way he said "we're" made her still even as warmth spread through her. Setting her mug down, she slid off the stool and rounded the island as he put the pan on a trivet.

She stepped closer to him and wrapped her arms around him, laying her head on his chest.

He hugged her back tight, his arms a comforting band around her. "What's this for?"

"Just thanking you again for helping me with this mess." They'd been texting for months, sure, and she knew him from his physical therapy, but this felt like a huge bound in whatever this thing might be between them. He was showing her exactly who he was—a good, protective man who made her feel safe on the most basic level.

"You don't have to thank me for this," he murmured against the top of her head, his breath warm, his grip comforting.

And for a moment his grip tightened, one of his hands sliding lower down her back as if he might…go lower, maybe clutch onto her ass.

She leaned back, looked up at him, but his expression was shuttered.

"You need to eat," he murmured, his hold loosening.

Eating was the last thing on her mind, but she didn't want to pressure him into anything. And right now he was throwing off confusing vibes so she sat again. "This smells amazing."

"It's one of the few things I can make so I at least do it well." He slid a cutting board with diced avocado, cherry tomatoes and feta cheese over to her before he started making his own plate.

She added all of it to her eggs. "So you're intentionally not telling me who you're meeting with, right?" He hadn't offered up the information and she wanted to make sure she was clear on that.

Dimitri grinned as he loaded up his own plate, and she really, really loved that grin. It made him look years younger. "I'll let you know everything I learn, but correct."

She wanted to push a little, to ask why he wasn't telling her, but figured he had a good reason for it. Instead, she took a sip of her coffee and eyed him over the edge of her mug.

He was so economical in his movements, so…hell, everything about him was sexy. The T-shirt he wore hugged all of him, showing off that he had indeed put in time at the gym this morning—and evidently a lot of mornings.

"I like it when you look at me," he murmured, glancing up and meeting her gaze.

She felt her cheeks flush, realizing she hadn't been very stealthy. Nope, she was just staring like a perv. "It's hard not to."

"I'm looking at you too, every chance I get." His words came out a low rumble she felt all the way to her core. "And if I didn't have to leave soon—" His phone buzzed and he winced slightly as he glanced down at it. "That's Juan. He's early."

She really wanted him to finish what he'd been about to say. If he didn't have to leave early, he'd…what? Strip off her robe right here on the countertop? *That* thought sent another spiral of heat rolling through her.

Yeah, it had definitely been too long for her. Way, way too long. And she realized that Dimitri was definitely the man she wanted to get back on the horse with.

"I'd give anything to know what you're thinking right now," Dimitri murmured before he leaned in, brushed his mouth over hers and headed for his front door.

She was thinking she'd like to kill her brother-in-law for his timing. Just a little.

CHAPTER SIX

"Thank you for seeing me." Dimitri sat in Viktor's home office, glancing around subtly, immediately noticing the changes from the last time he'd been here. Which had been... probably years ago. A lot had changed in that time. Viktor was now married with two kids—the second just born a couple months ago. There were pictures of his family and a couple drawings, definitely from his oldest, Lillian. Dimitri never thought he'd see the day when Viktor was so settled. Happy.

"Of course. I found out a lot in the last few hours. So did Lyosha." Lyosha worked for Viktor, had for years, first as his driver, then his head of security.

"I texted Lyosha a bit last night."

"I know."

Ah, of course he did. At one time Viktor had lived on the wrong side of the law. But now he was legitimate, had multiple hotels and businesses. And as far as Dimitri knew, everything he did now was legal. "How bad is this thing?"

"Not too bad. Not yet anyway. From what Lyosha dug up— and from what I confirmed independently—Kurt Ryba isn't close to his aunt. When he got tossed in jail, she let him rot. I believe she put out the word that he wasn't to be touched, but there's no love there. She thinks he's a fuckup and she's likely not wrong. He's her dead sister's kid and she had a lot of love for her younger sister—which is likely why Ryba is alive at all."

"Yeah, that's what I gathered too." Ryba had ripped off expensive cars, but the reason he'd been caught was because of greed and plain stupidity. And then he'd been dumb enough to get into a fight at a bar with some senator's son when he'd been out on parole. He'd been put away for a while because of that. Not long enough, however. "I can't believe he's out of jail."

"No shit."

"So he's not involved with Gorcyca, then?"

"No. I have heard, from a reliable source, that he's got some score lined up. A big one. He's trying to keep it under wraps but if I've heard about it...his aunt may have as well."

"Ripping someone off?"

"Likely, yes. No details on who or what, however. Just that he ran his mouth a bit, but wouldn't give up details."

Dimitri frowned. "What the hell could that have to do with Zamira? She hasn't seen him since her husband died and she says she barely knew him."

"You believe her?"

"A hundred percent. She's scared and confused right now."

"Her husband was a piece of shit."

"Yeah, that's what she said. Not in those words exactly, just that he wasn't who she thought he was when they got married."

Viktor lifted a shoulder. "We were all young and dumb at one time."

Yeah and he was glad to be past that stage. "I've got Ryba's contact info. I'm planning to call him." He wasn't asking Viktor for permission, wasn't asking anyone. But he'd worked for Viktor at one time and he respected the man's opinions.

"It's the smart move. It's what I'd do. Reach out, see what he wants with her and make it clear that she's under your protection."

Oh, he definitely would. And the selfish part of him loved having Zamira under his protection—and roof. "I'll need a neutral place to meet him, but somewhere that—"

"Meet him at one of my hotels."

"He'll likely know we're friends."

"Maybe, maybe not. He's younger than us by about a decade. And he never ran in our circles." There was a smugness to Viktor's tone that made Dimitri smile.

"True enough." Back when Dimitri had been working his own jobs, he'd never been into the smash-and-grab violence like Ryba. He'd taken the time to pick high-end jobs that had big payoffs. And he'd picked his targets carefully—rich assholes who'd been able to afford the losses.

"Just be careful and stay off Gorcyca's radar. She's a nasty piece of work."

"I'm not worried about myself."

Viktor watched him for a long moment. "What's going on with you and the Nowak sister?"

"The Nowak sister has a name—Zamira."

"I know. So?"

"We are…I don't know. I like her though." He scrubbed a hand over his face. "She's fun. And funny and smart and so fucking gorgeous I wanted to pummel all the assholes who checked her out last night."

Viktor let out a real laugh at that. "Welcome to the world of the insane. That's what happens when you fall for someone. You lose all sanity."

"Did you lose yours?"

"Of course I did…" He trailed off as his office door flew open.

Dimitri straightened, ready to go on the offensive, but sat back when Lillian raced in.

Looking half asleep, the six-year-old was wearing a long gown with a princess on the front, and her curly caramel hair was wild around her face. A white cat with orange stripes was with her, staring him down as if the little beast would tear Dimitri's head off. Good, the cat should be protective of Lillian.

"Daddy!" She jerked to a halt when she realized Viktor wasn't alone in the office. She looked between the two of them, her green eyes wide. Then she shoved her hands on her hips. "Dimitri!" Her tone was almost accusing.

"Yes, princess?" She was a small version of her mother, and adorable.

"Why are you here?" she demanded.

He blinked at her tone. She'd always had spirit but she didn't seem happy to see him.

"Baby girl," Viktor murmured. "Is that polite?"

Hands on hips, she turned to him and shook her head as she let out a big huff. "No it's not. I'm sorry, Dimitri. But no one tells me anything and I do *not* like it." She kept shaking her head as she muttered to herself and stalked out of the office, the cat racing after her.

Dimitri didn't bother biting back a laugh. "What was that all about?"

Viktor rubbed a hand over his face. "I don't know. She's been out of sorts since the baby was born. She's not jealous, not exactly, but it's been a big change and she doesn't like when anything out of the norm happens. It gets her agitated and cranky."

"Ah. When did you get a cat, by the way?"

"Not my cat." His tone was dry. "That thing is Lyosha's. She comes over here for playdates sometimes with Lillian, and yes, I said fucking playdates. With a cat."

Dimitri snickered. "My, how things have changed."

Viktor shot him a knowing look. "Things are gonna change for you too if you keep things up with Zamira."

"I know."

He quirked an eyebrow. "Do you know? Because she's a single mom of two kids."

"I'm well aware." And okay, it terrified him a little. He didn't know shit about kids, but teenagers were even worse. Or he assumed they were. People always said so. He'd been raised by a single mom who'd done the best she could so he respected Zamira even more.

Viktor just gave him a look that said he had no idea what he was getting himself into.

And his friend was right—he didn't really know, but he could see a future with Zamira and he wanted that. Because his instinct told him that if he didn't take a chance with her, he'd regret it for the rest of his life.

He glanced at his phone as it buzzed and the low-grade hum of tension eased when he saw the text from Juan.

All good, headed back to your place.

"Juan's on his way back to my place now with Zamira. Everything's good." For now. He knew Juan was more than capable and trained. He could protect Zamira.

But there were too many unknowns, and Dimitri wanted to be the one to protect her, to keep her safe. The thought of anything happening to her scared him far more than it should, considering they hadn't known each other long. But she'd gotten into his system.

"You want to stay for breakfast?" Viktor asked.

"No, but thank you. I'm going to call Ryba now."

Viktor nodded and stood. "I need to check on Lillian."

"I'll show myself out." He stood and held out his hand, grateful for his friend's help. Now, he would take care of this himself.

Take care of his woman.

Who wasn't actually his yet, but he planned on changing that soon if she was willing—and it seemed she might be.

Once he was in his SUV, he called the number he had on Ryba from a burner phone.

"Who the fuck is this?" Ryba answered on the third ring, sounding annoyed.

"You saw me with Zamira last night."

There was a slight rustling sound. "What do you want?"

"To talk in person about why you're hassling my female." He didn't like talking about Zamira like that, but Ryba was the type of man who would relate more to that kind of declaration than anything else.

"I just want to talk to her, that's it."

Yeah, right. "You can talk to *me*, and me only. Today." He rattled off the name of one of Viktor's hotels. "Four o'clock."

"I'll be in touch."

Not an answer, but it would have to do. Ryba would try to do a search on the number he'd called from, but that wouldn't give him anything. If he wanted to know what was up, he'd have to show up at the meeting.

There was nothing more he could do. Now Dimitri needed to get back to Zamira.

CHAPTER SEVEN

"So have you told anyone you're preggo?" Lizzy asked Angel as she grabbed a cupcake from the tray. "I mean, other than Juan, obviously."

Angel just shook her head at Lizzy, used to her friend's eating habits by now. "No, and it's only nine o'clock. Too early for cupcakes." She was setting up her bakery and Lizzy had decided to meet her here so they could chat about a surprise party they were throwing for one of Lizzy's sisters-in-law. She'd met Lizzy at a work thing with Juan about six months ago, and it was as if they'd been friends forever. Lizzy was a little bit older and a hell of a lot wiser. The woman seemed to have everything figured out. And if Angel was being honest, she was in awe of her.

"I have three kids—it's always cupcake time. Normally I don't even get any," Lizzy grumbled. "My kids devour them all like tiny little piranhas."

"Liar, liar. I know your man saves at least one for you at birthday parties."

Lizzy snickered and went to sit in one of the empty chairs away from the window. She had a habit of doing that, Angel had noticed. She never put her back to windows, and had to have a view of entrances. Angel's husband was the same way and she figured Lizzy had developed those habits after being married to a former Marine for a long time. Not to mention she worked in professional security—and was the head of Red Stone Security's cyber department.

"I've got a few ideas for the party if you want to hear them," Angel said.

"Definitely, because I have none. My idea consists of cupcakes and champagne."

Angel blinked, unsure if Lizzy was being serious.

"Oh, I'm serious," she said as if reading Angel's mind. "I figured you'd be good at this and I could get my sugar fix." Grinning, she took a big bite of the cupcake.

"Oh my God, you're so sneaky. But I don't mind because we get to hang out. I don't take orders well anyway so how about I just tell you what we're going to do and you make it happen?"

"Perfect. I swear we're a match made in heaven."

Angel just shook her head, but laughed. "So what's going on with your brother? Any news?" Lizzy had confided in Angel that her brother Benny had gone into WITSEC well over a decade ago and was now out. All threats to him were apparently gone and he was coming to visit. Lizzy was nervous but excited. It sounded as if her brother had been a screw-up—and Lizzy's husband Porter had some reservations about Benny in general.

"He arrives in a few days and Porter's starting to ease up a little. I can't blame him for his reservations, given the past, but it's been a very long time. Benny's thriving now and he's been clean and sober for almost a decade. All his friends are either in AA or NA and he's about to get married."

"That's fantastic news."

"Yeah, it really is. He still won't talk to my parents, but I don't care as long as I get to have a relationship with him." Lizzy polished off the cupcake, then ducked behind the counter. "You mind if I check out what you've got in the back? You said something about red velvet cream cheese, if I recall?"

"I saved half a dozen for you—and your kids. They better make it home."

"No promises." Lizzy hurried back into the kitchen so Angel started the espresso machine, getting ready for the morning rush.

As she began moving around, the bell on the front door jingled and she winced. *Oops.* She must have forgotten to lock it when she'd been getting the tables outside ready.

Two men strode in, scanning the place before the first one met her gaze. His eyes and expression were hard, but she forced a smile. Her bakery saw a lot of foot traffic and she was used to putting on her "shopkeeper smile" for people who were rude.

"Hey guys, we're not actually open yet for another ten minutes but if you don't mind waiting about five minutes, I'll get you set up. I just need to—" She broke off, heart constricting as she stared at the gun that suddenly appeared in the man's hand. *Ohgodohgodohgod.*

He moved forward quickly as the other one flipped the lock. She started to step back but he was so fast, shoving right past the countertop and wrapping his hand around her throat. "You're going to give a message to your sister Zamira for me," he snarled as he shoved her up against the metal prep area. It dug into her back as he got in her face. "Nod for me!"

She nodded as fear whipped through her, leaving her paralyzed. All she could see was the giant gun in her face, smell the coffee on his breath as he leaned in close.

"Drop your weapon now." Lizzy's voice from somewhere behind her was hard, angry, unlike anything Angel had ever heard.

The man turned slightly, then stiffened. "I can kill her before you shoot me."

Lizzy had a gun? *Oh thank God.* Angel remained still, trying to take small breaths. He still had his hand around her throat, but his grip had lessened at least. All she could think about was Juan, their baby, getting out of this alive.

"Maybe you can. But I can definitely kill both of you before you turn that on me. And say by some freak of nature that you get lucky and manage to kill us. My entire family will hunt you down and make you sorry you ever took your first breath." Lizzy's tone was quiet, lethal and more terrifying than if she'd been shouting. "You're also on camera, dumbass. You know who the Caldwells are?" Her voice went even quieter as she asked what was clearly rhetorical. "They will find you."

Angel could barely hear her friend at this point because her blood was rushing so loudly in her ears. But the man had taken a step back at least and was no longer touching her. She sucked in a breath but tried to make herself as small and quiet as possible.

"Hey man, we need to get out of here," the guy by the door said. "There are a lot of people on the sidewalk."

But the man with the gun didn't move, didn't take his eyes off Lizzy. And he was still pointing his gun at Angel. "I don't care who your family is. You give your sister a message." His voice shook with rage now. "She's going to give me what I want, what her husband owes me. Or next time I'll burn your little shop down with you in it. And I won't stop with you. I'll kill everyone in her family—starting with you." He backed up then, still keeping his gun pointed at her as he hurried out after his friend.

She heard the bell jingle, the door slam as she slumped against the prep station. Then Lizzy was there, pulling her into a hug. "You're okay," she murmured.

"I need to call Zamira, to warn her. Oh God, Juan—" He'd gone with her sister this morning to help Zamira pick up clothes because someone had been hassling her. Juan had made it sound like no big deal. Clearly it was a giant deal!

"I'm already calling him," Lizzy said as she hurried to the front door, locked it.

"I need to call the cops."

"No." Lizzy shook her head. "Not yet. We're going to handle this, and I'm getting a crew of our guys here today to keep an eye on you and the store. But you should call your sister, tell her exactly what he said to you."

Angel simply nodded and fished her phone out of her apron with trembling fingers. This wasn't something she'd ever imagined happening. And it had been so quick.

If Lizzy hadn't been here… She didn't even want to think about what could have happened. She just hoped her sister was okay—and was worried that guy might come back and make good on his promise.

CHAPTER EIGHT

"I'm so glad you're okay." Zamira clutched her cell phone tightly to her ear, ready to come out of her skin as she listened to Angel replay what had happened to her. Today could have had a much worse ending.

"Me too. Are you almost to Dimitri's?"

"Yes, and Juan is off the phone now," she said before she hit speaker. He'd been talking to Lizzy, who was with Angel.

"We're going to find that guy," Juan growled to Angel.

"I know," Angel murmured. "You'll be staying with Zamira, right?" she demanded.

"Of course, my love. But I want to pick you up as well—"

"No, no. Lizzy has people from Red Stone on their way over to watch me and the shop all day. I've got a handful of custom orders to make today. I can't cancel them, especially since Carolina will be running the front of the bakery."

Juan just frowned at the phone, as if he wanted to argue.

Zamira didn't want Angel there either. "Look, hon, maybe you should think about—"

"No way. I need to stay busy, to keep my hands busy, or I'll go crazy. And a couple of these orders are for quinceañeras. I'm *not* closing up shop. I'm not letting that asshole mess with my business."

"She's using that 'don't mess with me' tone," Zamira said, even though she wanted to argue, push for Angel to come stay with her.

Juan nodded, his expression pure frustration.

"I can hear you," Angel muttered.

"I know. I'm just worried and I hate that this happened because of—"

"You better not say because of you!"

Zamira sighed and glanced out the window, realizing they were near the turnoff to Dimitri's neighborhood. Some of the tension in her chest eased, knowing they were so close to his place. He made her feel safe in a way no one ever had. "I know it's not technically my fault."

"There's no technical. Now, what does this guy want?"

"No idea, but it's clear that I need to talk to him." Whether she wanted to or not. Dimitri had said he'd be setting up a meeting with him, but Zamira needed to speak to Ryba as well. Needed to figure out this mess. "Whatever he wants I'll give him." She needed her family safe.

"Well whatever happens, we've got your back."

"I know. I love you."

"I love you too. Now pass me to Juan."

Juan took her phone off speaker then held it up to his ear, started speaking quietly as he pulled up to Dimitri's gate. He punched in the code, and as he pulled through, her heart skipped a beat when she spotted Dimitri's SUV sitting at the end of the driveway, his garage door open. He must have just gotten back too.

Seeing him made her feel about ten times safer.

As Juan pulled up behind him, Dimitri got out of his vehicle, leaving it idling. "Hey, what's wrong?" he asked as she hurried toward him.

She quickly recapped everything as Juan parked.

By the time she was done, Dimitri's expression was thunderous. "Your sister is definitely okay?"

"If she wasn't, I wouldn't be here," Juan said as he approached, his face just as grim. "I want to hunt that bastard down and kill him."

Zamira had never heard Juan sound so serious, so lethal.

Dimitri glanced around before he motioned to both of them. "Let's get inside."

DIMITRI WAS IMPRESSED with how well Juan was holding it together, though the rage in his eyes was clear. Someone had threatened the man's wife with a fucking weapon. Had put hands on her. Dimitri rolled his shoulder once, all his protective instincts flaring up.

It took a certain type of monster to put hands on a woman. Now he had a better understanding of the man he was dealing with. Dimitri would not underestimate him.

"I made contact with Ryba," he said as they stepped into his kitchen.

"Before or after he threatened my wife at gunpoint?" Juan's jaw was clenched tight.

Dimitri looked at his burner phone. "What time did he show up there?"

"Right before nine."

"I called him right about then. He could have been leaving as I called. Or he could have gone in even after I did, wanting to threaten Angel to make sure Zamira does what he wants."

"He made a big fucking mistake." Juan's expression was dark, deadly.

"He did, but you can't go after him. Not yet. Maybe never. You know who is aunt is."

Juan gritted his teeth.

Dimitri looked at Zamira, who'd been quietly watching the two of them, worry in her expression. He didn't care if Juan was in the room, he pulled her into his arms, held her tight.

She wrapped her arms around him, buried her face against his chest. "I don't know if you should meet him now that we know he has a gun. Maybe we should just let the cops handle this?" she said as she looked up at him.

"No," both he and Juan said at the same time.

"Why not?"

"Even though there are two reliable witnesses, Ryba is still a wild card. He won't stay in jail for this, not at first. It'll take time to process him, then a trial date would have to be set and he'd likely be out on bail for that. That will give him incentives to go after the witnesses—Lizzy and Angel."

"He wouldn't get the chance," Juan said.

Dimitri agreed, but held up a hand. "We can't put that cat back in the bag. We have a chance to handle him ourselves. If, after talking to him, I realize you can't give him whatever he thinks you have, then we'll look at other options." And powerful aunt or not, Dimitri would eliminate Ryba if he remained a threat. And he knew Juan would have his six if it came down to taking more drastic measures.

"He's right," Juan said. "Even if this thing makes it to trial, a trial is a crapshoot. He wouldn't get much time."

Zamira nodded, but it was clear she didn't like it.

Dimitri didn't either. "I need a few minutes to make some calls." He looked between the two of them. "And I need to talk to you about something," he said to Juan.

"No way. If you're talking to him about this, I need to know too." Zamira placed her hands on her hips, fire in her eyes as she watched him.

"She's right," Juan added.

Damn it. "I know. I just wanted to talk to Juan about getting protective details on the rest of your family. I didn't want to worry you more."

"I'm already worried. For them, for my kids." Her face paled slightly, then she straightened. "But that doesn't mean I want to be kept in the dark. I deserve to know exactly what's going on."

"You're right, I'm sorry." He looked back at Juan. "We need people on all of her family members that are local."

"Already done—Lizzy Caldwell was there when shit went down. She's already called Porter. Security is being handled and it's on the house apparently. Angel's got two of the best at her bakery, which is the only reason I'm not racing down there now. Clarita, Carlos and the kids are at Mila and Lyosha's with a couple Red Stone guys—and his place is a fortress anyway—and Flora is at her boyfriend's."

Zamira simply raised her eyebrows at the mention of her mom, but didn't respond to the last part, though it was clear the boyfriend was a surprise.

"Good. Then I'm going to call Ryba." Dimitri's instinct was to handle this alone, to do it in his office, but Zamira was right—she needed to be part of this. Pulling out his burner, he made the call and wasn't surprised when Ryba picked up immediately.

"You fucked up," Dimitri growled.

"Fuck you," Ryba snapped. "We meet today at a place of my choice."

"The hotel is fine." He pushed because it would look weird if he didn't, but he'd known Ryba would never agree to the first place he picked.

"No." He named a museum not too far away. "It's public, so you can't try any shit."

"I'm not the one hassling innocent women in public. Or putting hands on them and threatening them with a weapon." He clenched his free hand into a fist, wishing he could pummel the shit out of Ryba. Dimitri could only imagine how Juan felt right now.

"One hour," Ryba said instead of responding. "Be there." Then he hung up.

Dimitri shoved his phone into his pocket. "I've gotta go. He wants to meet in an hour at a museum. You can't leave her," he ordered Juan.

"I'm not going anywhere, but you need backup."

Dimitri shook his head. "I've got that handled."

"Do you really, or are you just saying that?" Zamira asked. "Juan and I can go with you and—"

"No!" Dimitri said, once again in tune with Juan. He really did like the younger man.

"I don't mean show our faces, I just meant like, be there at the museum in case you needed us to call the cops or something." She twisted her hands in front of her, her expression pinched.

"I've got this covered, promise. I'm calling someone in for backup on the way." Lyosha. "I won't be alone." He pulled her into a loose embrace, savored the way she stepped right into his hold, as if it was exactly where she belonged.

She clutched onto him, and he knew in that moment he would do anything for this woman. "Please be safe," she whispered.

"I will." Ignoring Juan, glad that the other man had stepped back and was giving them at least the illusion of privacy, he brushed his lips over Zamira's.

He didn't deepen it, though he wanted to. Instead he just pulled her close again. He was definitely coming back to her— after he took care of Kurt Ryba.

CHAPTER NINE

Dimitri remained half hidden by the oversized sculpture of a shark, watching Ryba enter the room. There were five other people in the art museum's room featuring a local artist from a century ago. Ryba wore jeans, a T-shirt and boots. And he had a mean look to him.

Dimitri had known enough men like this one. Angry at the world. Entitled. Hell, he could have gone down that path himself at one time if not for luck and a different direction shoved in front of him.

Hands in his pockets, Ryba glanced around the room, looking at the other people slowly walking around, talking quietly. He was sizing them up, checking for threats.

When no one appeared to follow Ryba, Dimitri stepped out from behind the sculpture.

Ryba turned immediately, his gaze narrowing on Dimitri. He didn't back up, just eyed him cautiously, his mouth in a hard line as he looked him over.

Dimitri stepped forward, closing the distance between them.

Ryba looked around then and motioned with his chin toward an oversized window that had a bench in front of it. Overlooking a garden, sunlight streamed in, coating that part of the room.

Though Dimitri didn't like making himself a target, Lyosha had thankfully answered his call on the way here and was in the garden. Two of Viktor's other guys were also at the museum, covertly moving around.

"I don't even know your fucking name," Ryba said as he sat next to Dimitri.

"Dimitri Lenkov." He didn't love the idea of giving this dick his name, but he needed Ryba to look him up, to confirm that he wasn't law enforcement. It was the only way he was likely to get the guy to talk to him.

"You wearing a wire?"

He scoffed. "First of all, cops don't use actual wires anymore. And second, fuck you. I want to know why the hell you're harassing Zamira."

"She has something that belongs to me."

"What is it? She doesn't want anything to do with you. So let's clear this up today and everyone can move on."

"She knows exactly what she has."

"No. She doesn't. If you gave something to her dead husband, she doesn't have it. And she has no clue what you want. But if you tell me, she can look for it. She saved some of his things for their kids."

Ryba paused, eyeing him up and down. "You sure don't look like a cop."

"Because I'm not, dumbass."

Ryba bristled slightly. "You work for Red Stone Security?"

The question surprised him, but he kept his expression neutral. "Sometimes." He decided to go for honesty. This could be some kind of test.

Ryba frowned, looked away. "I didn't know a Caldwell was at the bakery this morning."

Ah, that was why he asked. "Otherwise it would have been

okay for you to rough up and threaten a woman? A petite woman who weighs maybe half what you do?" Dimitri's hands tightened into fists and he had to force himself to breathe evenly when all he wanted to do was choke the guy out.

"I didn't hurt anyone."

Dimitri wasn't sure if the denial was because Ryba thought he was recording their conversation or what. So he snorted. "Tell me what you want, and if she has it, you'll get it. You have to know that she wasn't aware of her husband's lifestyle. Not until right before he died in that accident."

Ryba shifted slightly, glancing away momentarily at the word accident, making Dimitri think Zamira had been right to question if her husband's death had been an accident at all.

"She should have what I need though."

"What. Is. It." Dimitri's patience was running low.

Ryba shoved to his feet. "I'm going to look you up, see if you're who you say you are. If you are, we'll talk again."

Dimitri was up before he'd finished, turning to face him and hoping Ryba saw the predator in his eyes. "You do that. And once you've done your homework, we're wrapping up whatever this is. The only reason you're alive right now is because of who you're related to."

A flash of fear flared in Ryba's eyes, but he quickly masked it and simply nodded before he stalked off.

Dimitri found it very interesting that Ryba hadn't mentioned his aunt. He could be avoiding talking about her because he was worried Dimitri was recording him. Or because he was afraid to use her name. Or hell, maybe they really had no relationship. Most criminals would love to throw around Irene Gorcyca's name.

It boded well for Zamira at least that Ryba hadn't brought up Gorcyca. If he wasn't working with her, and was working his own angle, it likely meant he had very little funds or backup. Which was probably what this was all about anyway. Money.

Had to be.

Ryba wanted something he thought Zamira had, something that would be worth a lot.

Unfortunately now Dimitri had to wait for Ryba to do his homework, to decide that he would meet up with Dimitri again.

While he was waiting on that to happen, there was something he could do. Glancing around, glad to see the room had cleared out, he called Zamira.

"Hey, are you okay? How did it go?" She was breathless, her tone worried.

"Everything's good. It went about as well as expected. At this point we're going to have to wait. But in the meantime, would you be willing to gather up all of Lucas's things? Juan and I will go with you to your house. I can't say for sure but I almost guarantee that Ryba is going to want to search Lucas's things and no way is that happening at your house. So I'd like to transport all his boxed-up stuff to a storage container in a neutral location. I know a guy who owes me a favor—I did the locks for his entire storage facility. He'll let us use one of his on a temporary basis." Dimitri hadn't called to ask yet, but he had no doubt.

"Wow, ah, yeah, thank you. I can gather everything and we can deliver it whenever you think."

"How about right now?" Dimitri wanted to be ready when Ryba called him back.

"Yeah, hold on." There was a slight rustling, then she said, "Juan said we can meet you at my place."

"Sounds good." Once they disconnected, he let Lyosha know that he was fine and to head out. He also thanked him for the last-minute backup.

He still hated what was going on, but at least they were headed in the right direction. Hopefully soon this would be a distant memory—and then he could convince Zamira to take a chance on him for more than a temporary fling.

~

"This is it." Zamira looked at the stack of boxes on her living room floor. She'd pointed out everything to Juan and Dimitri and they'd gathered everything and piled it into one place. Looking at all of Lucas's things, a weird pang hit her chest. Maybe not weird, but whatever it was, it hit her hard. She knew things wouldn't have worked out between them in the long run if he'd survived.

She'd been blind to all his faults until the end. But seeing all his worldly belongings laid out like this just made her sad inside. Sad for the man he could have been, sad that he hadn't gotten to see his kids grow up. Hell, sad that he didn't have a chance to grow out of who'd he'd been, because maybe he could have. "I don't want Ryba to just paw through all of it," she rasped out then swallowed hard.

Dimitri set his large hand on the small of her back, his touch comforting, grounding. "He won't, I promise. And if he doesn't find what he's looking for, we'll cross that bridge then."

Juan patted her shoulder awkwardly. "We'll load this up in the SUV. Why don't you just go rest for a minute?"

She really did adore her brother-in-law. Shaking away the melancholy, she grabbed the nearest box. "Let's just do this." She wanted it over and done with.

Dimitri plucked it from her hands, frowning, as if he didn't want her to do any of the lifting.

It should annoy her, but she liked that he was taking over. Just a teeny bit. It was nice to have a man looking out for her, wanting to take care of her. After Juan grabbed another big box, she lifted a smaller one and followed them to the back of Dimitri's SUV.

Suddenly Juan let out a short whistle and Dimitri turned, blocking her body with his as a luxury sedan pulled up next to her curb.

Oh God. She winced as her friend Mick Carmichael pulled up. He was a real estate agent she'd met a few years ago when looking at a property and they got together a few times a year, usually to go kayaking or boating. "He's a friend," she said to Juan and Dimitri, who both looked a little like they were ready to do battle with the newcomer.

She stepped around them, her sandals slapping against her driveway as she hurried toward Mick.

"I'm so sorry, I forgot to call you back," she said as he was stepping out of his car. And she'd forgotten to respond to his text as well. "I'm dealing with some family stuff, but that's no excuse."

Mick laughed slightly as he leaned against the trunk of his car, casual in light slacks and a polo shirt. He had a little gray coming in at the temples, peppering through his dark hair, and she knew he was one of those men who would age well, all distinguished and handsome. "I'm just glad you're okay. I didn't want to veer into stalker territory so I didn't call again. But…it's not like you to bail on plans and I was worried so I thought I'd run by and just check on you. Hopefully that's not too stalkery?"

"No, no, it's fine. I hope you at least got to take out your boat today?" He'd invited her to go out weeks ago and they'd planned on going today. He'd called this morning but she'd ignored it because Dimitri had gotten back from Ryba's. She'd been so consumed with fear and worry for Dimitri. Everything else had taken a back seat and she'd forgotten to cancel.

"Ah…" He glanced over at Dimitri and Juan, who were still loading up boxes, his expression curious as he shoved his aviators back on his head. "I didn't go, but it's not a big deal."

Okay, now she felt even worse. He'd taken her and the kids out a few times over the years and thankfully he was one of those men who was truly just looking for friendship, not more from her. "I'll make it up to you." She felt like a crap friend right now. She'd known Mick for years, and he was such a stand-up guy. He was also gay, so early on she'd known he actually wanted to be just friends with her.

"You don't need to do that. I'm just glad you're okay." He glanced at the men again. "You need help with anything?"

"No, just family stuff." That was all she could give him. "But I promise I'll be in touch and we'll set up another boating day." Even though she felt bad, she still needed him gone. They had to get all this loaded up and to that storage facility.

"Okay." He paused, shoved his hands in his pockets as he pushed up from the car. He opened his mouth once, as if he wanted to say more, but then smiled. "Let me know if you need anything?"

"I will. Sorry again," she murmured as he opened the driver's door.

"Everything okay?" Juan asked as she stepped into her foyer and found all the boxes in the living room gone.

Wow, they worked fast. "Yeah, I just forgot to cancel plans with him today."

"The boating thing?" Dimitri's voice was so neutral she couldn't read his tone. Or his expression.

"Yeah." She winced again, mentally kicking herself. Then she shook it off because she had more important things to worry about. "Who am I riding with?"

"Me." Dimitri's answer was immediate.

Okay, then.

"Unless you need me, I want to get to Angel's." Juan looked at Dimitri questioningly.

"We're good. Thank you for today."

"Yes, thank you so much." She pulled Juan in for a big hug.

"You're family," he murmured as he hugged her back. "And you're in good hands. I know this goes without saying, but keep me updated. I'm here for anything."

She nodded, wiping away unbidden tears. "Tell Angel I'll call her later. And tell her I'm sorry—"

"You've gotta stop with that. You didn't do anything wrong."

Yeah, she knew that but it didn't seem to matter. Ryba had

pulled a gun on Angel. Sweat broke out over the back of her neck as she thought about it so she forced the thoughts away, reminded herself that Angel was okay. "I know. See you soon."

He nodded, then said a few words with Dimitri and was gone.

"Are you ready to lock up?" Dimitri asked, his body language tense as he scanned her quiet street, clearly looking for a threat.

"Yeah." She plucked up the lightweight cardigan she'd forgotten last time from the rack by the door and stepped out with him.

Once they were on the way to the storage facility, she leaned back and allowed herself to relax. A little. Kind of.

"My kids texted. They're having a ball." That was one thing off her chest.

"Good." Dimitri reached across the center console and gently squeezed her leg. Heat punched through her at that simple touch, because all she could imagine was his big hand stroking over her everywhere when they had a lot less clothes on. "We're going to get all this figured out before they're home."

She nodded, desperately wanting to believe him. And if Ryba was still a threat, she wasn't going to let them come home. No one was going to hurt her kids.

CHAPTER TEN

"I love you both," Zamira said to her kids, looking at their faces on the video call.

Elisa's hair was windblown, strands coming out of her ponytail, and her cheeks were flushed. Andres looked much the same, his longer hair wild and out of control. And they had matching grins. Seeing they were having a good time, knowing they were far away from all of this and safe, made it much easier to bear.

"We love you too. And we're bringing you back a present!" Andres said.

Elisa elbowed him. "You're not supposed to say anything."

"Oh, right. We're not bringing you a present."

Elisa rolled her eyes.

"Hugging you will be my present," she said to them.

That made Andres laugh, and Elisa groan slightly. Even hearing her typical "teen groan," as Zamira had come to think of it, made her happy right now. When her kids were happy with the world, she could breathe easier. She worried for them on a daily basis of course, but times like this, knowing they were simply content, it made all the other crap in the world a little easier.

Once she ended the call, she flopped back on the guest bed, her mind working overtime. Ryba still hadn't called Dimitri, but it hadn't been all that long since they'd met at the museum earlier in the day. Not really. Just a few hours. But it was hard to be patient when she wanted to get all of this behind her, to *not* worry about a lunatic stalking her.

Dimitri was currently cooking them dinner and she would join him soon, but...she knew what she had to do.

First she called her mom, who conferenced in Angel, Mila and Clarita in moments.

"You better be coming over tomorrow," Mila said, her youngest sister's expression fierce as she spoke to Zamira. "I want to see both you and Angel for myself."

"We'll all be at your house," Flora said, clearly daring anyone to disagree. Normally Sunday get-togethers were at her mom's house, but tomorrow they'd decided Mila and Lyosha's would be the best location because it was the most secure.

"I'll be there. Dimitri too." She figured that was clear, but wanted everyone to know.

"So what's going on with you two?" Angel asked. "Juan wouldn't tell me anything other than you're staying with him."

"Who cares about that? How are you? Do you need to talk to anyone?" Zamira asked Angel.

"I'm fine. I was totally scared and freaked out but I swear I'm fine. I've had time to settle down and I need to tell you all something. I'm pregnant. I'm not showing but I'm right at fourteen weeks."

"Congratulations!" Zamira shouted. She knew how badly Angel wanted kids, and that she was having them with Juan was even better. Her awful ex had cheated on her and gotten his mistress pregnant with twins—after telling Angel he didn't want kids. Zamira was so glad Angel hadn't lost her chance because of an asshole.

Everyone else chimed in and soon things turned to talk of baby showers, which just made Angel laugh.

"It's my turn to throw the shower," Zamira finally got in. "So don't even think of trying to take over, Mama."

Her mom just grinned, then said, "I have news as well. My boyfriend is moving in with me. Abuelito is fine with it. Happy, even."

Zamira stared for a long moment. "Oh my God, this is serious, then," she blurted, stating the obvious.

Her sisters started firing questions at their mom, one after the other. Zamira soaked it up, just listening to everyone, a little shell-shocked that her mom was having a man move into her house. But her mama was a great judge of character so no doubt this was a good thing.

When there was a lull, Angel cleared her throat. "Do you have any news about...anything, Zamira?"

Suddenly that tension was back, coiled tight in her belly. "We're just waiting for a call. And by we, I mean Dimitri and me. Please thank Juan again for all he did today."

Her mother's face filled with concern. "Do you want to come stay with me?"

"Or me?" Mila chimed in.

"I'd offer but we're all over at Mila's already. And there's plenty of room here for you." Clarita grinned slightly. "The kids would love to have you here too."

"You guys are wonderful for asking but I'm good here, promise. Dimitri's house is huge and his guest room is very comfortable. It's like I'm on vacation." You know, except for the fact that someone had been stalking her, had attacked her sister to get to her and still wanted something from her.

"Guest room?" Her mama's eyebrows were raised, her tone all disbelief.

"Yes. *Guest room.* There's too much going on right now to even think about...whatever."

All her sisters just stared at her.

"Hey!" She couldn't keep the defensive note out of her voice. "No judging me."

"Not judging, girl. Just hoping you'll get back out there," Angel finally said.

Clarita nodded. "Yeah, you deserve it!"

Mila and her mom nodded and the conversation thankfully shifted in another direction. Once they started winding down, her mama told her to hold on after everyone else hung up.

"Are you sure you're comfortable over there?" her mama asked. "Because if you feel stuck—"

"Oh no, I don't feel stuck. I'm grateful to be here. More than that, I...really like him. Like a lot." It didn't seem to matter that there was so much about him she didn't know yet; Dimitri had shown her who he was with his protectiveness. There was still a worry in the back of her head that she was making another mistake, but she was trying to silence that voice. "I mean, he's kind of bossy, but it's nice to have someone stepping up, taking over." Looking out for her.

"Because you've been doing a lot on your own for thirteen years."

Her mom would understand—she'd done most of the heavy lifting even before their dad died. Raising four girls, helping out anyone in the neighborhood who needed it, working crazy hours. She was like a superwoman.

"True enough, but I've always had you and my sisters." They'd always helped if she'd asked—their help with childcare was the only reason she had a degree. She'd gotten scholarships, but that certainly hadn't covered childcare. So she would be forever grateful for the help they'd given her when she'd been a young mom. She knew not everyone had that.

"So he treats you well?"

"He does. He's cooking dinner right now." She grinned at that —it was really, really nice not to have to cook.

"I like the sound of that. Listen, my sweet girl, don't be afraid to take a chance because you got burned when you were young. You're older, smarter now. And even if he's not right for you, at least you'll try and know. You deserve the chance at something real," her mother said.

"So do you."

"I know. That's why I'm taking my next shot."

"You think you'll marry him?"

Her mom looked a little horrified at the question. "I don't know about that. Right now I need to see if we're compatible beyond the physical. He's still keeping his place until we decide if there will be a next step."

"Very practical."

"I insisted." Her mama shook her head slightly, a smile tugging at her mouth. "Now go, enjoy the rest of your night."

"I will." Or she would try. Even with the threat hanging over her head, at least she was under the same roof with Dimitri, a man who had brought out a side of her she forgot existed, made her feel alive in the most feminine way.

DIMITRI GLANCED over his shoulder the moment Zamira stepped into the kitchen, turned to face her. She was quiet so he hadn't heard her coming, but he swore his body was attuned to her presence.

When she was near, all he could think about was pulling her into his arms—and kissing her senseless. In loose pants and a fitted tank top, she looked relaxed and at home here. She'd left her hair down instead of pulling it back in a braid or ponytail and he wanted to run his hands through it as he claimed her mouth. And he really liked the sight of her being so comfortable in his house.

"Everything okay?"

She nodded, her gaze sweeping over him in a way he wondered if she was even aware of—with pure lust. "Yeah, just talked to my whole family. Are we still good to go over to Lyosha's tomorrow?"

"Unless I hear from Ryba, yes." And probably yes anyway. If he wasn't with her, then he wanted her with someone he trusted. And he knew she likely needed the support of her mom and sisters right now.

"Well, that answers my other question." She sighed and sat at the island.

He moved to pull the cork on the wine bottle he'd opened last night for her. "Would you like a glass?"

"Yes, please. I almost never drink, but with the kids gone I'm indulging a little bit."

At the word indulge, he wondered what else she might like to indulge in. Naked time with him, hopefully.

Damn it. He had to keep his head on straight. She was here because of a threat. She was counting on him to stay sharp.

"Thank you," she murmured as he slid the glass over to her. Then she glanced at the stovetop behind him. The empty stovetop. But she didn't say anything, which just made him smile.

"I overestimated the ingredients I had, so I called for delivery."

She let out a startled laugh. "That sounds amazing."

"Maybe not so amazing when I tell you that it's an hour wait."

"That's totally fine. This will tide me over." She lifted the glass in a half salute, making him smile.

Something he found he did often around her. *Smile.* She brought out a different side to him, made him want to open up to her in a way he never had with anyone. At the risk of being overly honest, he said, "I told you I was arrested when I was eighteen."

She straightened slightly, her dark eyes widening. "I didn't want to push, but I definitely remember."

He shoved out a sigh, wondering if he'd lose her by telling her who he'd once been. Praying he wouldn't.

"You don't have to tell me. It's okay," she said when he paused far too long.

"No, I want to tell you about my life—not just give you the curated parts," he added, mirroring what he'd said to her only a day ago.

Her full lips curved up. "I want to know everything you're willing to share."

He nodded toward the big glass doors that led to the patio and pool area.

She slid off her stool, grabbed her glass and walked out with him.

Once they were settled on lounge chairs in front of a small fire pit and he'd turned on the pool lights, he said, "I was arrested at eighteen because I got cocky. But it wasn't the first time I'd stolen something."

"Something?"

"Jewels this time. From a rich asshole—not that it makes it any better. I used to make excuses for my choices." He cleared his throat, watching her, trying to gauge her reaction. "And I'm not sorry for all of them."

"I like your honesty," she murmured before taking another sip.

"I was good at what I did. Fast, knew how to get in places quickly. And thanks to a good mentor and a knack for it, I was really good at disarming security systems and breaking into safes."

Her eyebrows raised, surprise clear in her expression. "That's…impressive."

He barked out a laugh at her response.

"I'm not saying it's a good thing, just impressive. Is that how you ended up owning a bunch of hardware stores? Oh my God, that's what you do for Red Stone?"

A small grin played at his mouth. He was glad she wasn't repulsed by him now. "Hardware stores are a necessity and a good way to stay legit. Once I got the capital, I started building them where there was a need. Then I expanded. And the Red Stone contracts came much later. Recently. But yes, that's part of what I do. Cracking safes isn't as common but it's still a skill they need and I have it."

"So what happened after you got arrested?"

"A judge gave me an option. I either got to join the military and 'straighten up' or I was going to jail. It wouldn't be a long sentence, I knew that. But I didn't want to go to jail, didn't want anything on my record. My mentor agreed, told me to join the military, and I'm glad I did. Now, anyway. I was pissed at first because back then I didn't see it as a real choice. But…if I hadn't, I'd have likely ended up back in jail or been killed."

She blinked.

"I was on a quick path to winding up dead. Sooner or later I would have pissed off the wrong people, or stolen from the wrong person." He was also glad to have joined the Marines for other reasons. He'd learned a lot of skills, learned how to survive in the worst conditions, and he'd met a handful of men and women he still thought of as family. "I didn't walk the straight and narrow after I got out—but I do now."

"Wow." She took another sip of her wine, watching him over the rim of her glass.

"Are you done with me now?"

She blinked in surprise. "No. Thank you for your honesty, it's just a lot. And it takes a lot to get on a different path and stay on it. I'm impressed."

He'd never thought about it like that.

"Can I ask what made you change?"

He paused, mulling over his answer. "It wasn't one thing. I did a lot of work for someone specific." He wasn't going to name Viktor because that wasn't something she needed to know and he wouldn't betray Viktor anyway. "When that individual started going legit, changing their whole life, I did the same. If I'm being blunt, I was getting older and I didn't want to constantly worry about getting caught. I wanted to carve out a real life and put down roots."

"That's really impressive."

He'd started to respond when his phone buzzed. His burner phone.

Zamira set her wine down suddenly as he said, "Ryba." Then he answered. "Yeah."

"So you're not a cop."

"Nope." At least Ryba had done his research. Hopefully now they could get this over with. "You ready to talk now?"

"I don't want to talk. I want what's mine."

Dimitri gritted his teeth, took a deep breath. He was about done with this guy. "And again, she does not know what you want. You won't even give a hint, so she can't guess." He looked at Zamira and she nodded at him. "But," he continued, "she's agreed to let you go through all of Lucas's things."

There was a beat of silence. "If I don't find what—"

"I don't give a shit what happens if you don't find whatever this thing is. You're not helping yourself by being so opaque and we're being more than accommodating. I've already moved all of Lucas's things to a storage facility so you can take your time going through everything. If you've done your research on me, you know I always keep my word."

More silence stretched out. "Where do you want to meet?"

"In the morning. Nine o'clock. I'll text you the address right beforehand. If you come armed or try anything, you'll regret it and this deal is off. Understand?"

"Yeah."

"I want to make sure that you do. I will hold up my end of this deal but if you fuck up again, you're not walking away."

"I got it." The phone disconnected.

Zamira shoved out a long breath as he set the phone down. He braced himself, wondering if now was the moment she got up and left. He'd been blunt talking to Ryba and he wasn't backing down. Not when it came to her safety. There were some things he would compromise with, but that wasn't one of them.

She rubbed a hand over her face, and to his surprise she got out of her chair and came over to his. She slid right onto his lap as if it was exactly where she belonged. "I need a hug," she murmured. "And I think you might too."

Ah, hell. He held her tight as she laid her head on his shoulder. He would definitely take a hug from her. And hopefully more. But he liked the feel of her curved up against him, plastered to him. She was fit and lean, but soft in the right places.

"What do you think he'll do tomorrow?"

"He'll show up. And I'm going to have backup. *We* are."

She leaned up slightly, her eyes wide as she watched him. And her mouth was perfect, begging for him to kiss. All soft and lush. "We?"

He held off kissing her just yet. "I won't allow him to come anywhere near you and I'm going to be armed—so will our backup. But yeah, I think you need to be there. He's looking for something and eventually he'll need to talk to you if he doesn't find whatever he's searching for. And I don't think he's going to. It's been over a decade. This thing might be gone."

"Yeah, I've been thinking about that too. Lucas's parents have some of his stuff, but it's mainly pictures and a few personal items from his high school days. Little mementos. What happens if... Ryba doesn't find what he wants?"

"We'll deal with that then. But he will not bother you." That, Dimitri would make sure of, one way or another.

Her gaze fell to his mouth then, the heat he'd seen earlier sparking wild. She sucked in a ragged breath and that was it. He moved fast, sliding his fingers through her hair, cupping the back of her head as he claimed her mouth.

She shifted immediately, moving from cuddling to straddling him in an instant.

He rolled his hips up to her as she settled over him. Just the feel of her on top of him, even with their clothes on, had him rock-hard. Hell, her cuddling against him had already gotten him hard. She was impossible to resist, especially now that he'd been honest with her and she still wanted him.

She'd *hugged* him, wanted to comfort him.

Fuck. It was impossible not to like this woman. More than like.

He forced himself to slow down, to enjoy the taste of her, but it was damn hard when she was starting to slide over his erection.

Oh, hell. They might have clothes on, but if she kept this up, it wouldn't matter. He hadn't come like this since he was a teenager.

But fuck it. As he teased his tongue against hers, learned her taste, he dipped his hand underneath her tank top. It'd been clear she wasn't wearing a bra earlier so he wasn't surprised when he slid his palm upward and got a handful of smooth, full breast.

She moaned into his mouth as he ran his thumb over her hard nipple. The little sound, the reverberation in her throat, had his cock going even harder.

Which shouldn't have been possible.

She rolled her hips against him again and he knew he wasn't going to last long—he didn't think she was either. He'd basically been walking around with a hard-on since he'd met her. For the most part he'd been able to keep it under control but now she was on top of him, moaning.

As he bit her bottom lip, he slid his other hand down the front of her pants—she didn't have anything underneath.

Okay, *now* he was the most aroused he'd ever been.

She practically shoved her hips at him as he cupped her mound.

He grinned against her mouth, loving that she was so into this, that she wasn't wearing any panties. And when he slid a finger through her folds, he was the one groaning at how slick she was.

"It's not going to take me long," she rasped out as she pulled back. Her cheeks were flushed as she watched him, her breaths sawing in and out.

"Good," he growled. He wanted to get her off, wanted her to experience a bit of pleasure—that was just the beginning. This would take off the edge. But he wasn't done after she orgasmed once.

No, he wanted all of her orgasms.

He slid his middle finger over her clit and she shuddered over him. He continued to tease her breast, then switched to the other, tweaking her other nipple between his thumb and forefinger as he watched her face, her changing expressions of pleasure.

She shuddered again, her eyes going heavy-lidded. She hadn't been kidding—she was so damn close.

He slid two fingers inside her easily and began rubbing the base of his palm over her clit in hard little motions.

And she went off.

Her inner walls clenched around him, hard as she jerked against him. She gripped his shoulder with one of her hands, digging her nails in. "Dimitri." His name tore from her mouth and the raw sound of it had him rocking his hips up against her even as he continued stroking her.

She arched her back, her breasts thrusting out as her climax hit hard. It seemed to go on forever, but simultaneously it was over too fast.

Breathing hard, she stared down at him as she still straddled him, her eyes heavy-lidded, sated. And to his surprise, she shoved her hand down the front of his pants and grasped his cock. Just like that, took what she wanted.

Then she started stroking as she watched him, kept her gaze pinned to his.

He gritted his teeth at the rush of sensation, his balls pulling up tight. He wasn't going to last and couldn't give a shit at the moment about anything other than her hand on him. "Harder," he rasped out.

She gave him exactly what he demanded. She wrapped her fingers tighter and kept going as she continued to watch him.

Something about the experience was more intense than he'd imagined, the way she was watching him, wanting him—*fuck*. He surged into orgasm, couldn't hold back any longer as she stroked him.

He let go of control, coming all over her hand and himself. Breathing unsteadily, he pulled her close so she splayed on him as the lounge chair fell back under their weight.

She looked down at him, her curls cascading everywhere as a very satisfied grin spread over her face. "We are not done for the night."

"Hell no," he growled, crushing his mouth to hers again—right as his stupid phone rang. The delivery guy.

She snickered as she looked down between the two of them. "Pretty sure we need to clean up first. Unless you want me to grab the food?"

He grasped onto her hips possessively. "No. You stay put, I'll be back." Then he kissed her again, already missing her even though he was only going to be gone for a few moments.

Yep, his bachelorhood was gone. Forever.

Because of Zamira.

CHAPTER ELEVEN

Dimitri felt Zamira stir against him, pressing her ass against his cock in her sleep. He knew she needed sleep; he didn't want to wake her up. But...for the last half hour she'd been pressed against him like this and he was rock-hard. With the two of them naked in bed together, of course he was.

After they'd gotten each other off on his back porch like teens last night, they'd had dinner, then fooled around a little. But nowhere near the level to where he wanted to be with her. Which was deep inside her as she wrapped her legs around him. After she'd fallen asleep naked against him, it had taken him a while to actually sleep.

Thin beams of light streamed in from the big window in his room, shooting little ribbons across his bed and the two of them.

"You're clearly awake," she murmured, her raspy voice filling the quiet room as she rubbed her ass up against him intentionally this time.

Grinning, he slid his arm around her, pulled her tight to him, savored the skin-to-skin contact. She was warm against him, the beat of her heart steady. "Hard to sleep with you next to me."

"Hard is certainly the right word." Her voice was tinged with amusement as he rolled his hips against her.

He slid his palm over her hip, down her abdomen and slowly cupped her mound as he nipped her earlobe.

She sucked in a breath, pushing back at him again.

He pressed his teeth down on her earlobe once, then said, "What are you thinking right now?" He wanted to know exactly what she wanted.

"That I don't want you to stop." She reached behind her, clasped onto his ass and tugged him against her.

His erection pulsed as he slid against her bare butt and back. *Fuuuck.* "Condom?" he murmured, feathering kisses along her neck. They'd talked last night—she was on the pill and they were both clean. But he wanted to make sure they were on the same page, that she had no regrets.

"No, if that's fine with you." Her voice was unsteady as he slowly teased his finger over her clit.

"Definitely okay." He started stroking her now, a little faster. She was already slick, but he was big and he wanted her primed and ready for him.

Arching her back, she continued holding his hip as he kept teasing her.

He liked the feel of her nails digging into him, enjoyed that bite of pain.

And he loved that she was trusting him with this—he knew it had been a hell of a long time for her. He wanted to make sure this was perfect for her.

Slowing his movements, he slid his hand up her abdomen and only stopped at one of her breasts, gently caressing her soft skin, tweaking her nipple.

He kept going until he cupped the side of her face, turned her to him.

Breathing unsteadily, she met his gaze, her eyes heavy-lidded as he claimed her mouth. The angle was odd, but he bit her bottom lip gently, savored the way she shuddered with pleasure.

While he wanted to push into her from behind, to slide right into her wet folds, this first time he wanted to have her stretched out under him, wanted all that skin to skin, and to be face-to-face so he could watch every expression flicker over her gorgeous face.

She must have had the same thought because she turned then, plastering herself against him as he pinned her beneath him.

Her legs spread wide as he settled his erection between her thighs. Angling himself at her entrance, harder than he'd ever been, he slowly slid inside her.

She rolled her hips up, made an impatient sound as she wrapped her legs fully around him, joining their two bodies completely. She was so wet there was no resistance.

Her inner walls were so tight around him, he sucked in a deep breath, mirroring her own breath as he pushed to the hilt.

They started moving at the same time, finding a wild, raw rhythm of pure pleasure. He lost himself inside her, loving every second of it. Savored every time she arched her back or rolled her hips up to meet his. This was Zamira, the woman of his fantasies, the woman he'd do anything to protect.

He reached between their bodies and she bit his shoulder with a surprised cry as he rubbed her clit.

So he didn't stop, kept teasing her until he could feel her climax building. Her inner walls tightened faster and faster as she reached her limit.

She let her head fall back on the pillow, her eyes a little wild. "Dimitri."

Oh, she was close, so damn close. He could feel it with every squeeze around his cock. Because he was close too, right on the edge, about to lose his battle to hold out.

Her eyes closed right as her climax hit, the little ripples around his cock intense as she surged into orgasm. *Yes.*

He dipped his head to one of her breasts as he continued thrusting, sucked hard on one of her nipples.

That set her off even harder. She grabbed onto him, digging her nails into his ass this time, and he let go, wanting to join her in orgasm. To come inside her with no barrier.

"Zamira." Her name came out a wild growl, a sound he barely recognized as he claimed her mouth in a rough kiss. He lost himself inside her, coming long and hard until the two of them were left breathing unsteadily in the aftermath.

He gazed down at her, traced over her lips with his finger, making her smile. He wanted to memorize every inch of her.

Then she bit his finger once and grinned. "That was a very nice way to wake up." She squeezed her inner walls around his half-hard erection.

He sucked in a breath and slowly pulled out of her. "Hopefully not the only morning we wake up like this." They hadn't talked about the future or "them." He'd been so focused on keeping her safe, and things had moved at warp speed the last couple days. He knew what he wanted but...she was a single mom. He didn't want to push her too hard, too fast.

"I should hope not," she murmured, her eyes going heavy with arousal as she kissed him again.

He immediately deepened it and rolled over so that he wasn't squashing her beneath him. And for a little while he didn't think about anything else but the very naked, amazing woman on top of him. Soon, they would have to leave—to take care of the problem plaguing her.

For now, he wanted her to feel only pleasure.

CHAPTER TWELVE

Zamira was glad that Dimitri was with her as they stood just inside the entrance of the storage facility. It was hard to believe that a couple hours ago she'd been naked, sated in bed with Dimitri.

Now...she was dealing with the remnants of her husband's past in a storage place with crappy air conditioning. To say that was frustrating was an understatement.

Two men had come with Dimitri—they worked with her brother-in-law Lyosha so she'd seen them around. And they were definitely armed. The bulges under their shirts made it clear they weren't bothering to hide the fact.

Ryba looked up at them, shot her a sharp glare as he closed another plastic bin—the final one. A shiver ran through her at the ice in his gaze. It didn't seem as if he'd found what he was looking for. And she had no idea what to do about that. Not when he wouldn't help himself by simply telling her what he wanted.

Dimitri stepped forward in a fluid movement. "Look at her like that again and I'm done playing nice."

Ryba's jaw clenched as he looked at Dimitri, his hands curling into balls. "It's not here."

"And you're still not going to tell us what it is?" Dimitri asked.

Ryba looked between the two of them. It was clear he wasn't talking.

Zamira took a breath. "Whatever you're looking for is obviously worth something. A lot of something, if the way you're acting is any indication," she snapped, drawing all his attention to her. "But if you'd actually think about this whole situation, you'd realize I don't have whatever it is you want. I live in a nice house, yeah, but I've got two kids who are expensive. Sports, clubs, braces, you name it. I've got bills just like everyone else! I'm not living a high life. We don't take crazy expensive vacations. I'm a mom, just raising her kids."

She didn't mention not having a mortgage—she didn't have one because her husband had taken out a life insurance policy. She'd wanted to make sure her kids always had a roof over their heads and she'd started saving for their future education.

"And you're not helping out at all in the information department. I've given you everything I could think of that belonged to Lucas. Everything I didn't donate. If he had something that was yours, I'd give it to you." She hoped he heard the truth in her words. Her kids' safety was worth everything. She would never put them in danger by withholding something.

"You should have answered my letters," he growled, then raised his palms slightly when Dimitri took a small step toward him.

"What did your letters say?" She wasn't backing down on telling him she hadn't received them. That was a lie she'd take to her grave.

He was silent a long moment, then he rubbed an agitated hand over his head. "Doesn't matter now," he muttered. "There's nothing else of his you're leaving out?"

She shook her head. "No."

Finally he nodded, his expression a mix of resignation and anger. "All right."

"Go wait in the SUV," Dimitri murmured without taking his eyes off Ryba.

She wanted to ask him to come with her, didn't want to leave him alone in this storage unit, but she wasn't going to argue. Not when he clearly wanted to have this out with Ryba here and now. "Okay."

DIMITRI NARROWED his gaze at Ryba, not liking the appreciative way he was checking out Zamira as she walked away. "Eyes on me." His voice was whiplash sharp.

"Sorry." Ryba shrugged, clearly not apologetic. "She's even hotter than she was a decade ago. Too good for Lucas, that's for sure—though he was a pretty boy, so I understand what she saw in him."

"And I'm thinking about not letting you walk out of this unit." Dimitri was done with this guy. He wasn't going to kill him—not unless he had to—but he wanted Ryba afraid of him.

Ryba's eyes widened, as if he just realized what he'd said. Or maybe he'd realized what a fine line Dimitri was walking right now. "No disrespect intended."

Yeah, right. This guy was either baiting him or just plain stupid. Probably both. "Are you going to bother her again?"

Ryba's jaw tensed, his forearm muscles flexing as he crossed his arms over his chest. He looked at the table of boxes and bins. "No."

"For some reason I don't believe you."

His arms dropped. "I won't!"

"She's under my protection—and Viktor Ivanov's." He didn't like throwing around his friend's name, but it was true. And Viktor had told Dimitri to make it clear to this little shit that if he made a move, Ryba would be up against the weight of Viktor.

Ryba's eyes widened ever so slightly. "He's not even in the game anymore." But there was definite fear in his pale blue eyes.

"You think he's any less dangerous now that he makes his money legitimately." Not a question.

Ryba didn't respond to that, just said, "Fine. We're square. She's off my radar for good."

Thank fuck. "If I see you anywhere near her, or think you're anywhere near her, you're dead. Keep your distance. Forever." *Or die.* "No one will ever find your body."

Ryba watched Dimitri for a long moment, then nodded, his expression confirming that he believed him.

Dimitri wanted to think that Ryba did, that he was too afraid to mess with her again. People didn't always act rationally, however, and Ryba was still a wild card. And unfortunately for Ryba, he'd pissed off more than just Dimitri. He'd pissed off Lizzy and Porter Caldwell with that stunt at the bakery. But Dimitri wasn't going to bring them up. He was worried if he did, it would spook Ryba into acting irrationally. If he was too afraid, he might think he had nothing to lose.

And people with nothing to lose were the most dangerous of all.

He followed Ryba out, watched him get into his car and drive off. Only then did he get in the SUV with Zamira.

"Well?" Her expression was tense.

"I think he's off your back for now."

"How sure are you?"

"I think you need to stay with me for the time being, and we're keeping someone watching your house." And if necessary, he was going to suggest that her kids stay with their grandparents even longer. But it hadn't come to that.

Yet.

She let out a sigh. "He's a problem," she finally murmured. "I wish I knew what the hell he was looking for."

"Yeah." A problem Dimitri was pretty sure he was going to

have to deal with. It didn't matter that Ryba had a powerful aunt—if he continued to pose a threat to Zamira, he would have to be eliminated.

The problem was making sure nothing fell back on him. Or Zamira. Because Dimitri wouldn't do anything to put her in danger.

CHAPTER THIRTEEN

"If you hurt Zamira, we will hurt you." Lyosha's voice was hard as he watched Dimitri across the table on his patio.

Most of the men were sitting near Lyosha's pool, but the women were all in the pool with the kids. He'd been invited here with Zamira so she could spend the day with her family, but he'd more or less expected a grilling from Lyosha, who was being overprotective of her.

Viktor simply glanced at his head of security, his expression neutral. Even in a bathing suit, sipping on a beer, the man had a deadly air to him.

Juan's expression remained stony as he stared Dimitri down. He'd wondered why all the guys had said they wanted to talk to him. Apparently it was to threaten him. Which he respected. Even if he was a bit confused, considering Juan had been giving him tons of unsolicited advice about how to win her over.

"We'll hurt your face," Carlos added, his words stilted and awkward as he attempted to threaten Dimitri. Then he winced.

Lyosha sighed, rubbed a hand down his face.

Viktor's lips twitched.

"You need to work on your threats," Juan murmured, shooting his brother-in-law a sharp look as he passed Lyosha a beer.

Carlos simply shrugged. "I'm a lover, not a fighter. And I've never threatened anyone before."

"Clearly," Lyosha murmured. "You're terrible at it."

"You better work on it, then," Viktor continued. "You've got two daughters who will bring boys home one day."

"So? I've got a son too. And I'm not going to be threatening *anyone* they date—I have no idea if they'll bring home boys, girls, or maybe—"

"Oh my God, we're getting off track," Lyosha muttered. "We're talking to Dimitri about his intentions with Zamira."

Carlos looked back at Dimitri and held out a hand, his expression apologetic. "I'm sorry I tried to threaten you. It's clear you care about Zamira. Even with what's going on, she seems really happy today. And if you hurt her, it's clear these guys will fuck you up and probably hide your body where it'll never be found. So I'd advise against doing anything to hurt her. I'm about to grab a beer, you want one?" The man was nothing like the others and Dimitri found he liked Zamira's brother-in-law—who spoke of her with the affection of a man who'd been in her life now for almost two decades.

Dimitri nodded, fighting a grin as he looked at the others. "So, you will all fuck me up if I hurt Zamira." He eyed Lyosha and Viktor, men he'd grown up around, respected. "What happens if she hurts me?"

"Then we will take you out and help you get over her," Lyosha said.

Viktor just shrugged in agreement.

"I would never hurt her." He looked away from them, their words beyond ridiculous. Which, he was pretty sure they all knew. He'd do anything to protect her.

His gaze was drawn to her in the pool as she tossed a volleyball to Viktor's little girl, who giggled and slapped at it wildly.

95

Dimitri shot Viktor a sharp look suddenly. "For the record, I remember when you first started dating Dominique. You...were not smooth with her." Talk about an understatement.

To Dimitri's surprise, Lyosha snickered. He was in full-on protective mode today, but that broke his hard exterior. "He was the worst. And now he wants to talk about feelings all the time. He does anything his girls ask of him."

"You still work for me." Viktor's tone was dry. "And you're no different with Mila."

"Nothing wrong with talking about feelings." Carlos—who Dimitri *really* liked now—rejoined them at the table. "If mi alma and I had talked about our feelings more, we would have had less troubles. Now we talk all the time and things are great. We're having more sex now than we did at seventeen." He looked very pleased with himself.

"He never stops talking," Juan murmured, though it was clear he was fighting a smile of his own. "Always with 'owning our emotions.'"

Carlos shrugged. "That's right. I'm going to be the type of father mine never was. I want my kids coming to me with their problems, not just to their mama. And I want my wife to know I'm always there when she needs me. I'm not going to be some emotionally stunted asshole."

Dimitri held his beer out to Carlos, nodded his thanks as he clinked his bottle against the other man's. "I'll drink to that."

"So." There was a shift in Viktor's tone then. "Ryba."

Dimitri's amusement about Carlos died as he looked at his friend. "I honestly don't know if he's still a threat."

"We will keep an eye on him, then," Lyosha said, even as he looked at Viktor for confirmation.

Viktor nodded.

"Porter Caldwell might take care of the problem for us," Juan finally said, setting his beer back on the table. "He has taken it very personally that some punk pulled a weapon on his wife."

Yeah, Dimitri was surprised Caldwell or his brothers hadn't had a "chat" with Ryba yet. Maybe they were biding their time. He didn't know them well, just by reputation more than anything. Though he'd had contact with Porter and Lizzy through his Red Stone contract work.

Viktor cleared his throat slightly. "I've spoken to Porter. He will not be making a move on Ryba. *Yet*. But he's got him under surveillance. His wife is angrier than he is and that's saying something."

"She can get in line." Juan looked over at Angel then, seemed to settle once he saw her sitting on the edge of the pool, her legs dangling in it as she talked to Zamira.

Zamira—who was walking sex in her little purple bikini.

Dimitri forced himself not to stare like a giant pervert, to not mentally undress her with his eyes. Hard not to, especially now that he knew exactly how she sounded when she came around his cock. How she looked beneath him as she climaxed.

"I know that look," Carlos murmured as he stood and patted Dimitri once on the shoulder before cannonballing into the pool —much to all the kids' delight.

"Yeah, so do I." Viktor's expression was unreadable.

So Dimitri slid his sunglasses on and stood, headed to the pool. He didn't want to talk about his goddamn feelings for Zamira with anyone. He barely had a handle on them himself.

She'd blown up his entire world and now he couldn't imagine her not in it. But he knew it wasn't that simple. Even without the Ryba mess, she was a single mom who had a busy life and a whole lot of responsibilities.

And he wasn't sure where he fit into everything. She hadn't given him an indication what she wanted either. Other than sex, which was great. For now.

But he wanted more from her.

CHAPTER FOURTEEN

Dimitri glanced up as Zamira stepped into his living room, a smile on her face. He loved seeing her smile, knowing she was a little more at ease after the day they'd had.

After dealing with Ryba, they'd gone to her sister and Lyosha's, and now they were back at his place. "I'm guessing your kids are good?"

"Very good," she said as she sat next to him with a smile. She kicked her feet up next to his on the big ottoman and laid her head on his shoulder.

She fit perfectly against him—perfectly into his life. Or that was what he was telling himself. Right now was just the two of them, but her kids would be back soon and...he wondered if she would want him to meet them. Technically he had, at the wedding, but that was before they'd started whatever this was.

"They're staying so busy, which is good. They don't have time to miss home and they're getting good bonding with their grandparents. I miss them though."

"Of course you do." He kissed the top of her head.

She settled against him. "I love this view," she murmured.

"Me too." It was his favorite spot, overlooking his pool and backyard area through the oversized glass doors. The view was part of the reason he'd bought the place. He didn't watch a lot of television at night, usually just relaxed by his pool with friends or by himself. "When I was growing up we had a small one-bedroom apartment," he said, deciding to tell her more about his past. He didn't normally open up to anyone. Viktor and Lyosha had known him growing up, and while he'd had it better than them—Viktor's father had been a violent psycho and Lyosha hadn't had any family—they never talked about their pasts. He wanted Zamira to know more about him though. Just as he wanted to know all about her.

"We?"

"Just me and my mom. She dreamed of getting us a two-bedroom place in a better part of town." That had been her dream, just a bit more space and a good-sized apartment pool. It broke his heart that her dream had been so damn small. "She tried so fucking hard for me, for herself. But...I don't want to say the system is necessarily rigged, but—"

Zamira snorted softly. "The system *is* rigged. If you're poor, with no built-in system of help, it's almost impossible to escape poverty. There aren't many ways out."

He kissed the top of her head. "Yeah, it really is. She worked two jobs all the time, but would pick up seasonal jobs too so it was often three jobs. And she never complained. She was born to immigrants who believed working hard was the only way to succeed. And to an extent, they were right. Hard work matters."

"It only gets you so far," she murmured. "I'm a single mom, yeah, but I've got a mom, an abuelo, and all my sisters. Back when I was in school, if my childcare fell through and I needed to be in class or at work, I had people to turn to. And I had health care through the school since I was a student. Without all that, my life would have turned out very differently. I had scholarships, sure, but without help..." She shook her head. "Life is hard without safety nets."

"It was hard for her, for us. But mainly her. I could see a way out because I was good at taking things. My mom…she didn't love it when I came home with things and couldn't explain where I got them. So I stopped bringing things home and just started paying her bills when I could. She wanted me to stay in school—and she's the only reason I got my high school diploma."

She glanced up at him in surprise. "You didn't go to college?"

"Nope. Does that matter to you?"

"Not a bit." She gave him a soft smile and laid her head back on his shoulder.

He'd never felt so settled with a woman before. Hell, never felt settled enough to open up so much about himself. "She died too young. Lung cancer."

"I'm so sorry." She squeezed his leg gently.

"Thanks. I was sixteen and it was far too advanced when they caught it. Her housecleaning job fired her but I was able to pay our rent and other bills while she was in the hospital. She never made it out of the hospital though."

Zamira looked up at him again, cupped his face gently. "That's very young to lose a mother."

Oh God, when she looked at him like that it was almost too much. Throat tight, he nodded. "You lost your father young too."

"Yes, but I had my family, my mama, we all had each other as support. It doesn't sound like you had anyone. And I'm not feeling sorry for you," she added. "Just sorry you had to go through that alone."

A tension he hadn't realized was bunching up in his shoulders eased at her words. She laid her head back on him again and he tightened his grip around her shoulders ever so slightly. "It was hard." When he'd lost his mother, he'd lost his only family. And looking back, it had hit him harder than he'd realized. "I went off the rails after she died. I stayed in school, graduated a year early only because I'd promised her. But also because I was focusing all my time on my other *job*."

"And then you got caught."

"Yep. Like I said, it's the best thing that happened to me. Until I met you."

Her head snapped up and she turned to look at him, her eyes searching. "That's a good line."

"Not a line." He was dead serious where she was concerned. "I like you a lot, Zamira."

At his words, a hint of panic bled into her dark eyes. And…he wasn't sure what to make of that. Maybe all she wanted was sex. That…would hurt.

"I like you too," she whispered. "But my kids will be home soon and I won't have all this free time."

"So?" Was she planning to pull the plug on them when her kids got home?

"So…you might get very sick of coming in last to soccer games and volleyball matches and—"

"Zamira, I get that you're a parent."

"You say that you do."

He tightened his jaw slightly. He knew he wouldn't be able to convince her with words, he'd have to show her that he wanted all of her. And yeah, it would be a huge adjustment but he was falling for her. Hell, he'd *fallen*. Hard. "Why don't we take this one day at a time, then?" he murmured, his gaze falling to her mouth. Though it was his instinct to take over, and the possessive urge with her was riding him hard, he held back. He wasn't going to scare her off.

The flare of panic subsided and she smiled. "That sounds good."

Turning toward her, he grasped her hips and tugged her onto his lap. They needed less talk and more naked time.

Grinning at him, she tugged her shirt off as she straddled him.

And after that, they didn't talk at all for a while.

~

"You didn't have to sit out here the whole time." Zamira tightened her robe around herself as she picked up her towel and T-shirt.

She'd decided to go for a late-night swim—and Dimitri had enjoyed watching. He was starting to understand how she kept up with her twins. She seemed to have unending energy.

"It was a nice show." He grinned as he plucked the towel from her. He'd also wanted to stay out here in case of any security breaches. His house and property were locked down tight but he was still on high alert after that meeting with Ryba. He wasn't sure if he trusted the guy to stay away. It was a fifty-fifty chance at this point and he couldn't risk Zamira's safety.

As they stepped back inside, he set the alarm automatically from his phone. When he started to put it away, it buzzed in his hand. It was ten, not obscenely late, but he never heard from any of his employees at this time of night.

"You feel like joining me in the shower?" Zamira asked as they stepped into his bedroom, already loosening her robe.

He'd moved her things into his room when it had been clear she'd decided to stay there. Right where he wanted her. He swept an appreciative gaze over her naked body as she dropped her robe and headed into his bathroom. He'd also noticed that she was a bit messy, the complete opposite of him.

"In a couple minutes," he murmured.

She just gave him a cheeky grin and moments later he heard the water start. He read over the text from Viktor, frowned. Some of it was vague, but not enough to misunderstand.

R has pulled in a small crew for a job. He's keeping it quiet. No idea if his relative knows about it. From the sound of it, he'll be moving on it soon.

That...could actually be a good thing. If he made a big score, he'd have what he clearly wanted. Money. *What's the job?*

Not sure. Yet. L has feelers out too.

Yeah, Dimitri did too, probably with the same people Lyosha

and Viktor were in contact with. If he could figure out what the job was, he could contact law enforcement anonymously and get Ryba arrested. It might not solve his problem forever, but it would get Ryba locked up for a while and take the heat off Zamira. *Thanks for the update.*

He received a thumbs-up so he set his phone down, contemplating all his options. Some darker than others. There were certain lines he hadn't crossed, but he realized that to keep Zamira safe he'd cross every single one.

Shoving that thought aside—for now—he started stripping. He wasn't going to waste one more second not being inside Zamira. Things might not work out between them—her kids would be home soon and she might realize she didn't want him complicating her life. She might decide he was too much work, so he was going to enjoy every moment he had with her until that moment happened.

Even as he hoped that time never came.

CHAPTER FIFTEEN

Zamira pushed out a slow breath as she lowered herself onto Dimitri's hard length. Crouched on top of him, she balanced her body just slightly above him as she took him inside her again. She was barely touching him with her body—just his cock was inside her as she straddled him. He felt amazing like this, stretching her just right, and she knew he loved it.

All the muscles in his neck were pulled tight, his expression dark and hungry as he clutched onto the headboard.

She'd asked him to give up a little control this morning and he'd agreed. At this point she was pretty sure she'd pushed him to his limit. Her limit too, if she was being real with herself.

Her inner walls clenched tight around his thick length, and in this position his cock slid over her G-spot every time she lowered herself on him. She'd never been so wet, so aroused in her life.

"You're killing me," he gritted out, his eyes bright with hunger.

Yeah, she was killing herself too, in the best way possible. It was difficult to believe she'd only been here a couple days, but since they'd started having sex she was possessed with the need to get as much as possible.

It was like she was making up for all the years she'd gone without. And Dimitri was better than anyone she'd ever been with.

"You love it," she murmured, using her thighs only to lift off him, keeping a perfect balance as she raised herself until just the tip of him was inside her. Right about now she was grateful for all her workouts and kitesurfing because he felt amazing in this position.

"Fuck yeah I do." The veins in his neck were visible as he rolled his hips up, trying to thrust deeper.

And she caved. Twenty minutes of teasing him, and herself, was too much for her—her nipples were rock-hard, begging for his touch, his mouth, and she was right on the edge of climax, had pushed herself too far.

But she wanted to drag out every second of pleasure as long as possible.

She sank down on him and planted her hands on his muscled chest, then started riding him.

He unwrapped his fingers from the headboard, moving lightning fast as he grasped her hips and started thrusting hard. It was as if she'd unleashed all his restraint.

She loved the way his fingers dug into her hips, the bite of pain and pleasure mixed as he thrust deep over and over in a fast rhythm.

Already trembling with need, she wasn't surprised when her climax started to ramp up, the stimulation against her G-spot exactly right.

He let out a grunt of pleasure as she started clenching around him, driving into her as he suddenly rubbed her clit.

The extra sensation was too much, sending her into a free fall of pleasure. "Dimitri," she cried out, the pleasure punching through her, taking over all her nerve endings as she collapsed on top of him.

Still hard inside her, he ran a hand down her back, her ass, slapped it once in a way that had her tightening around him despite her recent orgasm. There was so much for them to explore and she wanted to try everything with him.

He eased her off him and kept holding her hips as he moved in behind her.

Though her legs were shaky, she pushed back against him, already having learned that she liked this position with him too—who was she kidding, she liked all of them.

He guided himself into her from behind, his breathing raspy, and thrust hard.

She leaned forward, loving how deep he went each time. When his climax finally hit, she shuddered along with him, loving the way he held on to her so tight, the way he smoothed a hand down her spine as he came down from his orgasm.

She simply loved everything about him.

And that scared her on a deep level, one she didn't want to think about too much. Right now it was just the two of them in a sort of cocoon. But that wouldn't last. Nothing ever did.

Her life could be chaotic on a good day and she worried that once he saw the real her, what her life was truly like daily, he'd decide he liked uncomplicated, easy.

Something she would never be.

DIMITRI WONDERED if it was possible to die from pleasure as he lay in bed with Zamira. Sunlight streamed in from the slightly raised Roman shades. It was still early, the sun just having risen a couple hours ago.

And he still needed to feed her. But he was enjoying her lying naked on him after their morning bout of sex.

She was insatiable, something he understood was because it had been a while for her. And he certainly wasn't complaining. But he wanted more than physical and hoped she did too.

"I kinda want to lie here all day," Zamira murmured.

"Fine with me. Or we could use the pool later."

"If I can get up." Her words had a drowsy quality and he could actually hear the smile in her voice. "It's weird to not have any plans. Good weird, but weird."

"What would you have been doing today if you weren't here?" He stroked a lazy hand down her spine, enjoying the sensation of simply touching her.

"Hmm. It's Monday so…I had breakfast plans with Angel today. Canceled, obviously. Then I'd planned to kitesurf for a while, and then dinner plans with a friend from my book club."

"You're in a book club?"

"Yep. And a kitesurfing club too."

He laughed lightly. "You are an interesting woman, Zamira."

She shrugged and kissed his chest once before laying her head back. "Are you hungry? Because I could definitely eat."

"Me too. I—" He paused at the sound of his burner phone ringing. Only Ryba had that number.

Zamira shot up, clearly recognizing the ringtone as well.

He slid from his bed and hurried to his dresser by the big window, grabbed it. "Yeah?"

"I've been thinking," Ryba said.

Hopefully he didn't hurt himself. "About?"

"Zamira owes me and I'm going to let that debt go if you help me with a job."

"You're out of your fucking mind." She didn't owe him shit and Dimitri certainly didn't.

"According to what I've heard, you used to be the best."

He snorted. He still was.

"And I have a job coming up where I need someone just like you."

"Yeah, what is it?" He wasn't going to help the guy, but he needed more details before he could cut the guy off at the knees. Needed to know what he was up against.

Now Ryba snort-laughed. "We'll talk in person. And if you

don't do it, our deal is off and your girl isn't safe. Neither are her kids. I'll text you where to meet." He hung up before Dimitri could respond.

Rage popped through him, but he took a deep breath. Losing control wouldn't do any good, wouldn't help the situation.

"Dimitri?" He turned to find Zamira standing at the foot of the bed, her discarded robe wrapped loosely around her, her dark eyes worried.

"It was Ryba," he said, confirming what she had to know as he looked at the incoming text. He winced at the location. A strip club. But it made sense Ryba would want to meet there—people usually weren't allowed to use cell phones. Not obviously anyway because of worries of client privacy. And it would be loud, a good place for a private conversation. "He wants to meet."

"Don't go."

He sighed. "I have to." He had to at least try to get Ryba off Zamira's back, to figure out what he was planning.

She stepped up to him, placed her hands on his chest. "We should call the cops."

Gently, he took her hands and tugged her close. "They can't do anything. He hasn't done enough to warrant anything from them."

"He held Angel at gunpoint."

"I know. And I also know he won't stay in jail for long if he gets arrested for that. It'll be a slap on the wrist. He might do a few years because he already has a record, but I doubt it. Then he's back out again. I want to at least meet with him and find out what he wants from me." If he could figure out what this upcoming job was, he could involve law enforcement and get Ryba put away for a very long time.

"I think we shouldn't take the risk." Panic laced her voice. "He could easily hurt you."

He pulled her into his arms and was glad when she leaned into him, laid her head on his chest. "If I don't at least meet with him, you'll never be safe." He didn't mention her kids because he didn't want to scare her even more. "I'm doing this."

She pulled back, her expression fierce. "You need backup, then. You're not going alone!"

"I know."

Some of her fire seemed to fade. "You've got someone in mind?"

"I do. A couple people I work with at Red Stone. I'm going to feel them out, see if they're up to helping." They had the type of skill for something like this and wouldn't be recognized by Ryba if they were spotted.

"And if they don't?"

"They will." If they didn't, he'd reach out to Lyosha again, but he wanted to handle this with unfamiliar faces. Ryba wouldn't recognize Isa or Graysen, likely wouldn't even notice them at the club.

Zamira gritted her teeth, then pulled him into a fierce hug. "I hate all of this and I hate that you're involved," she said against his chest.

"I know. But we'll work things out." No matter what.

CHAPTER SIXTEEN

As he sat at the curved, cushioned table in the dimly lit bar area, Dimitri glanced around the strip club. As far as clubs went, this one wasn't a dive, but it still had that skeevy feel to it. At least they had security for the workers, though from his easy entrance a few minutes ago, not good enough.

He'd strapped a knife to his calf and had a small pistol sheathed against his ankle. He was surprised he hadn't been frisked, but that told him Ryba had simply chosen this place because it would be easy to talk here. Not because Ryba had connections here.

Though he could be wrong, and he wasn't going to underestimate Ryba.

He had a feeling Ryba was going to underestimate him though. The fact that he'd called Dimitri and made threats this morning told him that he already had. He was also clearly desperate, which made him dangerous.

As he scanned the place, he let his gaze roll right over Isa and Graysen, a married couple he worked with at Red Stone Security. Isa was his boss when working jobs and she was very good at getting into computer systems undetected. He'd seen her work and it was magic. She would have been a great thief.

A steady thump sounded over the speakers, a newish song he vaguely recognized as a man said, "Give it up for Candy, everyone!"

Dimitri tuned out the rest of the intro as his waitress walked up, set his drink on the table. It was way too early to be drinking, but he needed to blend in until Ryba got here. Little bastard.

"You want to start a tab or look at the menu?" The woman, whose nametag simply said Red, wore a French maid's costume that left nothing to the imagination and looked bored as hell.

He set a twenty on the table and slid it over. "Keep it. I'll let you know if I decide to order food."

Her eyes widened slightly but she pocketed the bill. "If you do, the burger is the only good thing on the menu," she murmured, then winked.

He gave her a half smile that quickly died as Ryba swaggered over. He had on jeans, a T-shirt with no sleeves and a stupid trucker hat. It was as if he was trying to look like a douchebag.

Dimitri might not care for Ryba's aunt, but the woman at least had style and sense.

He did a quick scan of the other man, was pretty sure he had a weapon tucked under his T-shirt. The bulge was too visible. Looked like a knife. Dimitri had also seen two men walk in with him and veer off to another booth, so Ryba wasn't alone.

"I'll have what he's having and make it quick," he called out to the waitress, who stopped to glare at Ryba.

"Take your time," Dimitri said to her. Then, as Ryba sat, he shook his head. "You think it's smart to be rude to the people who have control over your food or drinks?"

"She knows I'm just joking." He sat on the opposite side of the booth and spread his arms out on either side of the back.

Okay so he was playing "big man" right now. When in reality he was a tiny piece of shit.

Dimitri kept his expression neutral. "Talk."

"Since your woman lost what she owes me, you're going to help me pull off a job. It'll be quick. In and out. And your payment will be that your girl walks away free."

Dimitri watched him long enough that Ryba started to squirm in his seat. "What's the job?" he finally asked. He couldn't appear too eager, but he needed more details.

"No way. I'll tell you at the last minute. That way you can't screw me over."

"I don't need your job or the money. If I'm involved in this— and I'm not saying I will be—I need to know what to expect. What kind of tools I'll need."

He shrugged. "Standard ones."

God, this guy really was stupid. Dimitri took a deep breath, prayed for patience. The waitress appeared then, slammed the drink down so that it sloshed a little, then tossed napkins at Ryba.

"Ah, come on, Red, don't be like that," he whined.

In response, she turned away from them, her little skirt flaring, revealing her thong and mostly bare ass. Ryba stared at her, practically drooling like a dog.

"Focus," Dimitri snapped out. "There are no standard tools. And if this is how you do business, I'm not working with you. And I'm certainly not working for free."

"It's not free if you and your girl get to live."

"You really are fucking stupid," he murmured.

"Excuse me?" Ryba sat up straighter, leaned forward, and out of the corner of Dimitri's eye he saw the two men shift slightly in their booth.

He also saw Isa and Graysen tense at theirs, but they didn't get up.

With the many mirrors in this place, it was easy to spot any potential threats. No one else even hinted at moving. The rest of the men in this place were all transfixed on the only woman currently dancing. There were barely dressed cocktail waitresses walking around, but it was a scant crew working given the relatively early hour.

"You heard me. And I only work for professionals."

"Fine, fine." Ryba held up his palms. "You'll walk away with a cool mil. Tax free, no one knows about it, and it's only a couple hours of work. Can't beat that."

Nothing was ever that easy, something Ryba *should* know. Maybe not, considering how much jail time the guy had done. "How much are you walking away with?"

Ryba shifted a little, took a sip of his drink, winced. "Pure vodka?"

Dimitri lifted a shoulder. "How. Much."

"Five mil. But that's because this is my idea. And I've set everything up. And," he added, looking around, "no one will ever report anything because the item is stolen to begin with."

Dimitri raised his eyebrows. "That's interesting." And also potentially dangerous if the person they stole from was a criminal. This sounded far too messy.

"I swear, this is the easiest job you'll ever do. And everyone I've talked to says you're a total pro and—" Ryba straightened suddenly, fear bleeding into his gaze.

Dimitri turned slightly, then did a double take. Despite being in this shitty place away from Zamira, he let out a short laugh, surprised to see a very old acquaintance. Whereas Dimitri had been good at taking things that didn't belong to him, Maxim had been very good at convincing people to pay back money they owed. After a career fighting, he'd worked for a loan shark in Miami decades ago, but had eventually gone on the straight and narrow. "Maxim."

The man gave him a wide smile and pulled him into a hug when Dimitri went to shake his hand. "It's so good to see you!" His voice boomed, as loud as Maxim was big.

Dimitri laughed as he stepped back. "You too. I thought you'd moved."

"I did. But my daughter goes to college here so..." He shrugged. "I'm back for a week and stopped by to see a friend."

Dimitri glanced around, saw one of the bouncers watching Dimitri with annoyance. "Friend, huh?"

Maxim shrugged, then laughed. "Eh, an old boyfriend. He says you are far too handsome, doesn't like me talking to you." He looked back at the bouncer, smiled, then faced Dimitri—sparing Ryba a surprised look. "You're meeting with this one?" he asked in Russian. "He's no good. Very stupid."

"I'm well aware." His tone was dry.

"Ah, okay. As long as you know. You're busy, I can see. If you're free, let's meet up before I head home. I must return to Chicago soon."

"Sounds good." He held out his hand, hoping to avoid another bone-crunching hug from a man who had at one time been a professional fighter turned bruiser for hire.

Maxim grinned, as if reading his mind, and shook his hand before stalking off.

"You know Maxim Novikov?" There was a hint of awe and likely fear in Ryba's tone as he sat back down.

"It would appear so."

He let out a short curse. "He knows my aunt."

"Is that a problem?"

"No, of course not."

Oh, but it was clear that it was. "Does your aunt know you're running a job here in Miami?"

"It's not in the city limits and...no." He cleared his throat, then straightened. But some of the swagger from before was gone.

Hmm, not in Miami. That was at least something, though not much. Dimitri needed to get into Ryba's phone, or more accurately, Isa needed to clone it.

But Ryba needed to unlock it in front of him for her to do so. Isa had told him that was the only way she could grab his information. So far Ryba hadn't made a move to touch his cell.

"Then we need to stop talking right now." This was good news for Dimitri. If Irene Gorcyca didn't know about this, then Dimitri had just validated that Ryba didn't have his aunt's go-ahead for this job. Which meant Ryba was trying to keep this from his aunt. All he'd have to do was threaten Ryba right back. He decided to push Ryba a little. "And if you walk away, I won't tell Irene you approached me about a job in her territory, without her knowledge."

Ryba sat back, his expression dark as he looked over at his friends, then at Dimitri. "No."

Surprise punched through Dimitri. "No?"

"That's right. You care about the widow too much. You can tell my aunt if you want, but bringing her into this will just get messy. For both of us. All it'll take is a stray bullet and Zamira is dead. Gone. Her kids left without a mom."

The little shit was right. Dimitri had to actively resist the urge to lunge across the table and choke Ryba out. Dimitri didn't have much leverage because he cared too much for Zamira. Would do anything to keep her safe. And he couldn't try and bluff when it came to her safety. So it looked as if he'd have to do this the hard way—to agree and then involve law enforcement. Or agree, then kill Ryba. Something he would only do if he was forced.

It could get messy but it was better than letting Ryba's aunt get involved. He didn't want to be on her radar in any way. "Then I want details. I'm not walking into a situation blind. There's a reason I've stayed out of jail."

The tension in Ryba's shoulders loosened slightly as he sat forward, ready to talk. Just as suddenly, he let out a short curse, his gaze straying behind Dimitri.

Using the mirror behind Ryba, Dimitri glanced up and saw a

man in a suit walking toward them. Because of the angle, he couldn't see the guy's face.

But as he got closer, Dimitri bit back a curse of his own.

Irene Gorcyca's second-in-command.

Things had just gotten a lot more complicated.

CHAPTER SEVENTEEN

Dimitri nodded politely at the man as he approached the table. "Gareth."

"Dimitri. Been a long time. Surprised to see you here." Though he was in his fifties, maybe even sixties now, he was fit and definitely armed. And he'd been helping Irene run her show for close to forty years.

Dimitri shrugged, knowing anything he said would be a mistake now. He and Gareth weren't friends, never had been. But they'd both run in similar circles a couple decades ago even with the age difference between them. Dimitri had gotten out of his illegal lifestyle, but Gareth would never quit working for Irene. He was loyal to the bone.

When Gareth turned toward Ryba there was more than a hint of derision on his face. "Your aunt is here. She wants to speak to you. Both of you," he added to Dimitri.

Ah, hell. Yep, way more complicated. But Dimitri simply nodded and gave a subtle signal to Isa and Graysen that everything was fine as he slid out of the booth. He didn't want them calling for backup. Yet.

Hopefully he wouldn't need it.

"How've you been?" he asked Gareth, who led them toward the back of the establishment, in the direction of a darkened hallway. He'd done enough research that he knew Irene didn't own this place. But people talked and she must have had eyes on her nephew, keeping tabs on him. She'd want to know why he was talking to Dimitri.

"Can't complain. Last kid is finally graduating college this year." He gave a small smile as they reached the exit door.

"Nice, congrats." The conversation was all mundane and polite yet Dimitri knew that if the situation changed, Gareth would put a bullet in his head no problem.

Outside, the sun beat down on them, the thump of the music fading as the door clanged shut. Ryba had been very quiet as he walked, likely thinking of a way to spin this to his aunt.

And an SUV was waiting, an Escalade with tinted windows and flashy rims. Irene was no doubt inside.

"You know the drill. Phones and weapons," Gareth said as they approached the vehicle. He paused, motioned for Dimitri to spread his arms.

"I'm armed," he said. "Two weapons, left leg."

Ryba looked at him, shocked.

Yeah, absolute dumbass. He should kill the guy and just rid the world of his stupidity.

Gareth was not shocked. He took the weapons and his cell phone, put them in a small cloth bag and motioned for them to get in the back seat. Dimitri was a little surprised Gareth hadn't checked Ryba, but clearly he must not view him as a threat.

Inside, Irene was in the passenger seat and a man with dark sunglasses was driving. The driver didn't turn toward them, but Irene did, smiling warmly at him. She'd always had a knack for that—a warm, easy greeting when he knew she was a shark who pounced at the mere scent of blood in the water. In her sixties, she looked to be maybe late forties. Her inky black hair was cut into a bob, highlighting her sharp cheekbones and full mouth. A beautiful woman, at any age. Her looks and charm had fooled a lot of men to their deaths—it was why she'd stayed alive and under the radar for so long.

"Dimitri Lenkov. It has been so long."

He smiled back, even though tension balled tightly in his middle. "Irene, you're looking lovely as ever."

"Thank you. That's always nice to hear." She made a quick motion with her hand and her driver pulled out of the alley.

"Just speaking the truth," Dimitri said, paying attention to the direction they headed. "You haven't aged a day since I saw you last."

She laughed then, a robust sound. "I always did like you. Now, why are you speaking with my idiot nephew?"

Ooooh.

Next to Dimitri, Ryba stiffened, but didn't respond. Even so, Dimitri could practically feel the rage and humiliation dripping off him.

"Before you respond, I'd like to remind you that even though I like you, it won't save you if you lie to me." Her voice was neutral, calm. She hadn't changed at all.

"He came to me with a business proposition. I turned him down." He lifted a casual shoulder. It was the truth. He certainly wasn't going to bring up anything to do with Zamira.

She turned slightly in her seat, finally looking at Ryba, annoyance clear in her pale blue eyes. "You weren't very subtle when asking around about Dimitri." She made a tsking sound as she shook her head.

"I was working on something big. I wanted to have all the details ironed out before I brought it to you, that's all. I wasn't going behind your back." There was a hint of desperation in his tone.

Eyebrow raised, Irene looked at Dimitri.

He had to play this carefully, walk a thin line of truth. "We hadn't gotten that far in discussions since I turned him down flat.

I'm not interested in running any jobs. I've been out of the game a long time anyway. I'm out of practice." He gave a quick, self-deprecating smile. "I like my life the way it is. No complications."

"Hmm." She faced forward then, ordered her driver to make another turn, this time into a parking lot. "It's my understanding that you occasionally work for Red Stone, so you're not completely out of practice."

"It's just contract work, very small jobs." He glanced down the strip of shops, recognized the area. Irene owned at least a few of the businesses in this strip, maybe all of them.

Her driver pulled up to another SUV.

"Tell me about the job," she ordered Ryba.

Ryba shot him a nervous glance, then dove into his plan to rob someone in Fort Lauderdale. Someone he knew had seen something interesting on social media—on an influencer's channel. Some woman had been at a house party and taking videos, and in one of the videos a very valuable painting that had gone missing a few years ago was in it. Could be a fake, but Ryba didn't think so since the video had recently been deleted.

Irene tapped her fingernail against her leg as she listened. Once Ryba was done, she said, "Very interesting." Then she knocked on the window twice. "Thank you for bringing this job to me. Well done." Her tone was too icy to be sincere. Clearly she had no respect for her nephew.

Ryba's door opened and one of her men nodded at him to get out.

"You stay," she said to Dimitri. "We have more to discuss."

Damn it.

Once her nephew was gone—shoved into the back of another SUV—she let out a sigh. "He's such an idiot," she muttered, making her driver laugh, the first sound he'd made. "It's a shame we're related." She turned back to Dimitri, her expression speculative now. "How on earth did you get on my nephew's radar?"

He just shrugged.

She watched him closely, her eyes narrowing slightly. So maybe she didn't know about Zamira—and Dimitri wanted to keep it that way.

Then she huffed out a breath, leaned back in her seat and looked out the windshield. "It's actually a good idea. A really good job. I'll need to do some more research but you will be part of the crew."

He gritted his teeth, knowing that if he said no right here in the SUV, he risked his life. He could take Irene on, but there was no guarantee her driver wouldn't simply turn and shoot him. And he couldn't see the guy well enough from this angle. "I'm out of the game."

"Even so, you will do it. I'll be bringing in outsiders for this one, no one linked to the city. You're a good choice since you're not active and you look like you've gone straight from the outside. There will be no fallout from law enforcement." She nodded, her mind clearly made up. "Yes, this is a fantastic idea."

He had no choice but to say yes, at least for now. "I don't do weapons and I won't be party to hurting anyone. I'll only work this if no one is home. No one is hurt. Period. And I would prefer not to work with Ryba." Not that he thought that was actually on the table, he just wanted to be clear.

"I know your reputation," she said dismissively as her driver pulled back into the parking lot for the strip club. "And I'm shipping Kurt up to Pensacola. He's useless and I want him out of my hair."

She hadn't actually agreed to his terms. But at least she wasn't killing him and she was getting rid of Ryba. For now. Unless Pensacola was code for "getting rid of completely." Which wasn't a terrible thing.

"I'll be in touch," she added as his door was wrenched open from the outside, dismissing him.

Gareth handed him the cloth bag with his weapons and stepped back, letting him out.

He got out and slid into the front seat of his SUV but didn't start the engine. Instead he watched as Irene's driver pulled away, then he texted Isa.

Then he did a sweep of his vehicle, making sure nothing explosive had been planted on it. That had been a slim possibility but he wanted to check anyway. When he got home, he'd check it for trackers thoroughly. Irene would know where he lived so if she had planted one, he wasn't worried about her knowing the location.

That was already an unfortunate reality.

Once he was done, he called Zamira, needing to hear her voice.

Thankfully, she answered right away, relief in her voice as she said, "Dimitri."

He felt the punch of his own relief. "I'm okay." For now.

CHAPTER EIGHTEEN

Dimitri kept an eye on the rearview mirror, wasn't surprised when the SUV that had been blatantly following him passed by his driveway.

He paused, watched as his gate closed, then steered down the driveway. He'd known Irene would have someone follow him, but had expected them to be stealthier. Apparently they didn't care about that. She was sending him a clear message—she was watching. As he pulled into his garage, he texted Isa again, then hurried inside.

Zamira was waiting in his kitchen and jumped off the stool the second he stepped into the room. "I'm so glad you're okay."

He'd told her what had happened—a condensed version. "Totally fine, and it sounds as if Irene is sending her nephew away so you won't have to worry about Ryba for the time being."

"But now you have to worry about a bigger threat."

"She doesn't seem to know about you at least." He eased back, cupped her cheek gently. Irene was smart, and if she'd known about Zamira, Dimitri was certain she'd have subtly threatened her. Or not so subtly. "This is going to be okay."

A chime sounded from the front of his house and she froze.

"It's just Isa and Graysen, the people I told you about."

Expression still tense, she nodded. "Right."

He brushed his mouth over hers before he hurried to answer the door.

Isa, a petite woman with jet-black hair, stepped in first, her husband Graysen right behind her. He dwarfed her with his size, but Isa had a fierceness to her that had gotten her far at Red Stone Security. There was a reason she'd recently been promoted to head up an entire division. Though today they were casual in jeans and T-shirts to blend in with the afternoon crowd at a strip club.

"Thank you both for coming," he murmured, locking up behind them. "Were you seen coming in?"

"No, we waited until your tail left," Isa said.

"Were you able to clone Ryba's phone?" He figured it was no, but asked anyway.

"Unfortunately no, but I did record most of your conversation with him before that guy took your phone."

At least that was something, but not much. "This way," he murmured, leading them to his kitchen, where Zamira was still waiting.

After making quick introductions, the three of them stood around the island. It was clear Zamira was too tense to sit and he figured Isa and Graysen weren't staying long. Just enough to go over everything.

"When that Gareth guy took your phone, I kept recording and I actually got something," Isa said, jumping right into it. "Gareth made idle talk with who I assume was one of the bartenders at that club, but then he made a few phone calls. It sounds like it's about that job Irene wants you to take part in."

"Anything I can use?"

Isa lifted a shoulder. "Not really. It mostly lines up with what Ryba told you and his aunt. Sounded like he was simply confirming the story and securing the people they want working with you."

"You get any names?"

"No, unfortunately. Just codes. The recording is on your phone so you can review it, see if you recognize any code names."

"Any mention of Zamira or Ryba?"

"Nothing about Zamira." Isa gave her a small smile before turning back to Dimitri. "But he did mock Ryba a bit. There's no love between aunt and nephew."

"So she's really sending him away?"

"Yeah, she has some low-level stuff that she wants to keep him busy with for a while. It's a plus for now. He'll be gone for a bit."

"Involving the police is definitely out, right?" Zamira looked between them, even though it was clear she'd already answered her own question.

"Yeah. If I do, she'll know it was me," Dimitri said. "Or she'll suspect it. And she could come after me—and you, if she realizes you mean something to me." Irene didn't seem to at the moment and he was hoping to keep it that way.

Zamira's expression softened as she watched him. "I don't want you to risk any more than you already have."

"That ship has sailed," he murmured, hating the tension vibrating off her.

"They want to move fast," Isa said, drawing their attention back to her. Graysen hadn't said anything yet, but he nodded his agreement.

Fast could mean as early as tonight, but he doubted it. That was too quick for a job Irene would want done right. And while she could be a violent psychopath on occasion, she was smart. She planned things out. They should have a couple days.

Which meant he'd have to be a step ahead of her. "I'll do the job but I'm going to bring some others in on my end." If possible. He wasn't walking into a trap.

"I'm definitely in," Isa said.

"Me too," Graysen said. "We're not letting you handle this alone."

Zamira shoved out a breath of relief and picked up his hand, squeezed.

"Thank you both," he said.

They nodded, then after some more talking, he walked them out.

When he stepped back into the kitchen he was surprised when Zamira basically threw herself into his arms, her eyes glistening with tears. Everything he knew about her said she didn't cry often. He hated the sight of them, wanted to cause Ryba physical pain because he was the root of her pain and tears.

"I hate that you're in this mess because of me! And I'm not crying," she added as she buried her face against his chest. "These are expressions of my anger."

Despite everything, a laugh escaped as he held her close. "This isn't your fault. It isn't anyone's fault. It's bad luck. And I'm not walking into this thing blind. I have an idea of who we're going to be targeting. And…I'm good at getting into places I shouldn't. I won't be taking any unnecessary risks. It's not as if Irene wants us to fail. So she'll do what she has to, to make sure we're prepared."

Zamira's cheeks were wet as she looked up at him. "If anything happens to you…" Her voice trailed off in a whisper.

Dimitri cupped her cheek, wanting to take away all her worry. He liked that she cared so much about him though. He was totally gone for her, no coming back from this now. "Nothing will happen to me. I've got a plan."

He was going to do the job, then afterward he was going to have a sit-down with Irene—with a handful of others. She was never going to bother him again. And if he could pull everything off, she'd end up in jail for the rest of her life and never think of him again. He wouldn't even be a blip on her radar. But even if he couldn't send her to jail, he could still get her to back off.

Zamira grabbed his T-shirt and tugged him down to her, her expression a little wild, hungry.

Groaning, he shoved everything else to the back of his brain as he claimed her mouth, then claimed her right on his kitchen floor.

He wasn't sure when it had happened but he'd completely fallen for her. Zamira had changed everything for him, the way he saw his future—hopefully *their* future. But with her stress levels already so high he knew he couldn't say anything to her, couldn't push her.

He wouldn't add any more to her plate.

But he would take care of her until this mess was settled. And then he planned to lock her down forever. If he could convince her to take a chance on them.

A real one, not just something based on sex.

Though that was incredible too.

CHAPTER NINETEEN

Dimitri's door chime sounded and he jerked up, saw the time. Five a.m. His place had a security gate. No one should have been ringing the bell.

"Dimitri?" Zamira rasped out, rolling over on her pillow. "What is that?"

He grabbed his phone, pulled up the security app—Gareth, Irene's guy, was at his front door. "Get dressed now. Irene's guy is here. I can't know for sure but he's going to make me go with him." Ignoring her gasp, he looked at all the other cameras, doing a quick sweep. No one else appeared on any of the feeds. Okay, that was good. Irene hadn't sent a team to kill him. There was no reason she should, but it eased some of his tension.

Zamira sprang out of bed, still looking half-awake as she stumbled to tug on a pair of shorts from the floor, then a T-shirt.

The chime sounded again.

Damn it.

Dimitri tugged on jeans and a T-shirt, grabbed his burner phone, put it into his front pocket, then shoved his real phone down his pants. "I don't know exactly how this is going to play out. But I've been in this situation before. He's likely going to grab me, take me with him because the job is happening sometime today. In the past I would get pulled into jobs and have all my communication cut off without warning. It's a way to eliminate people calling the cops." Or a backup crew to rip off the original crew, but he wasn't going to get into all that. The details weren't important.

Zamira's eyes were wide now, her breathing unsteady. "What do I do?"

"You're going to hide in the guest closet," he said as he went to one of his drawers, pulled out a small pistol. "I'm not planning on letting Gareth in here and I'm going to set the alarm when I leave. But you'll stay in hiding until Lyosha gets here," he said as he handed the weapon to her. "You'll stay put."

"Lyosha?" She shifted slightly on her feet, looking dazed.

He hated that he had to go over this so fast. Hadn't expected this to happen today. He'd just met with Irene yesterday afternoon. She was moving way too fast for something like this, but he should have been better prepared. That was on him. "Call him now. And if anyone but me or Lyosha opens that closet door, shoot."

Eyes wide, she nodded and raced to the guest room as he made his way to the front door.

The chime went off again right as he yanked it open. "What the hell are you doing?"

"Give me your phone." Gareth's voice was cold, emotionless.

Yeah, this was what he'd been worried would happen. Dimitri yanked out his burner phone, slapped it in Gareth's outstretched hand and started to step back inside.

"Nope. We're leaving now." He moved forward, as if to stop him.

Dimitri moved fast, slamming him face first against the brick of the entryway, and yanking his arm behind his back. "I'm getting my fucking shoes on," he growled. "And coffee, since you couldn't see fit to call me first."

Gareth let out a low growl. "Shoes are fine. No coffee. You've got two minutes."

He let him go and slammed the door in his face. Then he raced back to the guest room. "It's me."

Zamira opened the closet door, her eyes still wide, but she looked more awake now. "I talked to Lyosha. He's on his way here."

"Good. Go with him and stay safe."

"You're the one who needs to be safe," she said, the words a clear order.

"I will." He kissed her quickly, because he couldn't not.

Then he ran back to his office, grabbed shoes and his already packed bag of tools and clothing appropriate for break-ins.

Before he opened his front door, he set his alarm, then stepped out to a scowling Gareth.

The man started to reach for his bag but Dimitri shook his head. "You break any of my tools, you buy 'em." He might be here against his will, but he couldn't appear as if he was anyone other than he truly was. And he didn't let people push him around.

At least he knew that Lyosha was on his way to pick up Zamira. And that she was armed in case anything happened beforehand.

Gareth looked through his bag, feeling the lining carefully, then said, "Spread your arms out. You know the drill."

Rolling his eyes, he did as ordered and was glad that Gareth avoided his crotch—where he'd tucked his phone.

Heart rate kicked up, he finally followed Gareth to a waiting SUV. "Can we stop by a Starbucks?" he growled as he hopped in the passenger seat. "I need coffee."

Gareth just grunted.

Which better be a yes. He just hoped he could pull this off. More than that, he hoped Zamira made it to safety. That was the only thing that mattered.

Once he knew she was safe, pulling off a job would become a hell of a lot easier.

~

Zamira jumped when her phone buzzed.

I'm here. Coming inside. A text from Lyosha.

Her heart rate was still out of control and had been since she and Dimitri had been woken up in a rush. She still hadn't come down from that scare, was still riding that wave of fear.

She opened the closet door as she heard the little chime announcing the front door had been opened.

"Zamira?"

"I'm here!" She set the pistol on one of the dressers and hurried out into the hall.

Lyosha looked as if he'd been awake for hours and was dressed for battle in dark tactical pants—and had a gun in one of his hands. He swept a gaze over her quickly as he tucked his weapon away. "You're unharmed?"

"Yes. Scared out of my mind though." For herself, for Dimitri.

Lyosha reached out and gave her the most awkward pat on her shoulder. He was like a robot. "It will be okay."

Oh, sweet mangoes. She knew how much this man loved her youngest sister, and he was wildly protective of all of them. But his attempt at comfort made a laugh escape, a nervous, out of control sound that bubbled up inside her. Oh no, she couldn't let all this worry leak out. If she did, she'd be a mess. She had to keep herself under control because that was what the situation called for. Dimitri was taking on a whole lot right now for her, so she would keep her shit together.

His expression softened. "I swear, he'll be fine. We have a plan. Are you packed?"

Plans were good. "Yeah, mostly. I can have my stuff ready to go in a couple minutes. Also, there's a gun in there," she said,

131

motioning to the guest room door. She wasn't touching it again but figured he might want to secure it.

He nodded, moving into action as she made her way to Dimitri's room. She'd only been here a couple days, even if it felt like a lifetime. So she hadn't unpacked her stuff, she'd just been living out of her suitcase. She gathered up her toiletries and most of her stuff because she wasn't sure how long she'd be gone.

Wasn't sure of anything.

And that...hit her hard as fear for Dimitri weighed her down.

As she rolled her stuff into the hallway, Lyosha was there, Dimitri's gun tucked away. He immediately grabbed her stuff and hauled it toward the front door.

She knew she needed to leave with him, to get to safety, but leaving felt like she was abandoning Dimitri somehow.

CHAPTER TWENTY

Dimitri resisted the urge to pace in the large open warehouse. He'd been dumped in it hours ago along with one woman and two men. Everyone for the job later tonight.

Irene's people had moved fast, bringing everyone here around the same time so it had been coordinated. He vaguely recognized the woman and one of the men. But the man with the blond hair who was around five foot ten he'd never seen before.

No one was using their real names—he was Joe, the blond was Don, the woman was Ava and the other man was Eli. All short and easy to say over their comms if necessary.

At least the place they'd been ordered to wait was furnished and had a small kitchen with food and drinks.

Eli was currently watching a soccer game on the television in one corner while Don was doing sit-ups. Ava had done yoga for a while, then she'd started pacing. Though it didn't look like nervous pacing, more like the kind you did when you were practicing counting the number of steps you took.

From the very short dialogue he'd had with the others, Eli was the getaway driver, Don was the lookout who would be monitoring the neighborhood and the cameras in the house. He would also act as a distraction in case law enforcement was called.

Dimitri would be breaking into the house—Gareth had already provided the type of security system installed, and while high-end, he had the tools and tech to crack it.

As soon as he was inside, Ava had orders to grab the painting. Dimitri also had orders to do a quick sweep looking for anything else of high value.

A decade ago he'd have loved the thrill of this job, though he'd have never worked for Irene. No, he'd worked for himself and Viktor. No one else.

Right now he didn't feel that rush, not like he once had. He wasn't afraid either. This was...unease. Worry for Zamira. He hadn't had a chance to call her yet and he needed to try before they got hauled out of here. He hadn't been able to contact Isa and Graysen either, but that ship had sailed. He would have liked to use them for backup, but that wasn't happening now.

He finished another water bottle, set it noisily on the counter of the small kitchen area. He'd finished a few bottles in a row so it would be obvious why he was going to the small bathroom in the far end of the warehouse.

Not that he needed an excuse, but he had no clue if they were being watched. Probably were. And he wanted all his actions to be as normal as possible.

Once he was inside the eight-by-eight space, he glanced around, gave it as good a look for cameras as possible. Paint was peeling off the walls and there was a rusty color ringing the interior of the toilet. Dust covered the back of the tank. There were no exterior windows, no way to escape. Not that he was thinking of it. Not yet anyway.

After he was as sure as he'd ever be, he texted Zamira. He thought about calling but it was too risky his voice would carry. The warehouse beyond was mainly open space with the exception of the bits of furniture and the kitchen area.

I'm safe, he texted.

Thank God! She responded immediately. Then, *This is Lyosha now* immediately followed her text. *We know where you are. Keep your phone on you if possible. If not, ditch it and be safe. As soon as the job is over, we'll pick you up.*

He sent back a thumbs-up emoji, then *take care of Zamira, going dark.* He hated that he couldn't talk to her, couldn't hear her voice, but it was probably better this way.

He had to keep his head in the game. Had to stay alive.

As he started washing his hands, two sharp pounds sounded on the door. "Come on!"

He swung it open, found Gareth standing there, his expression unreadable. "Time to go."

Dimitri kept his expression just as neutral and grabbed a paper towel, started drying his hands. "I'm ready."

DIMITRI CROUCHED in front of the keypad by the glass back door. The entire house was dark, with just the pool area slightly lit up. From his intel, the owner had decent security, but leaving lights on was always a good idea.

He and Ava had already taken out the sensor lights, and the two men were waiting back in the SUV.

"Clear on our end," Don said through the comm line.

"I'm almost in." Dimitri was holding his small device up to the keypad, waiting for it to cycle through possible codes.

Click.

The lock snicked open. If there'd been biometrics it would have been a different story and he'd have likely just gotten in through a window. A hell of a lot easier.

He and Ava stepped through the back door, both whisper quiet as he now stood in front of the alarm keypad.

A little *beep beep beep* had started, letting him know his time was limited. He pulled out another device, clicked it right over the panel, then started working on his tablet.

"Go, get the painting," he said softly as he worked.

Ava didn't respond, simply raced away into the dark home.

"Vehicle approaching," Don said into the quiet. Then, "It's nothing. They kept going, pulling into the neighbor's drive now."

"I've got eyes on the painting," Ava whispered.

Dimitri shelved all that as background noise as he continued working, his fingers flying across the keyboard. He'd written this code himself, had put it to good use plenty of times during his contract work. And he'd been practicing today at the warehouse.

But there was a sense of urgency that never happened until he was working a real job. With real consequences.

Beeeep. The alarm clicked off suddenly.

And he shoved out a sigh of relief. He unhooked the device, then tucked it back into his duffel bag along with his other tools. "We're in and I've made it look like the system is resetting itself after an update," he said along the comm line. "We've got three minutes before we need to reset it, or if someone is monitoring the security system, they'll know something is off."

"Cameras are fine," Don said. "Nothing's changed and no one will know I'm in the system."

In the past Dimitri had worked the security cameras and the alarm system but Irene had wanted someone else handling the cameras. Which was just as well. They hadn't had enough time to do recon and he was literally depending on someone else who'd gathered the intel.

He didn't like doing a job like this. It left far too much up in the air. But he was wearing gloves and a mask so if someone tried to screw him over and use video footage of him breaking in here, it wouldn't exist.

Still, he was very aware of the clock ticking away, letting him know he needed to be fast.

Hurrying after Ava, he used a flashlight to guide his path. He found her in a large study, rolling up the painting she'd cut straight from a gilded frame and putting it into a container.

"You see a safe?" he asked even as he started making his way through the room, looking under the other hanging paintings.

"Nope." She snapped her fingers once, then lifted a hand to her ear.

Using his flashlight, he saw her motion that she was shutting off her comm.

He muted his. "What's up?"

"Take the painting, make sure it gets to Irene. I'm not getting back in that SUV."

The hair on the back of his neck stood up. "Why not?" He actually wasn't planning on it either, but he didn't like new things cropping up during a job.

"Because I don't trust Irene and I know you don't either."

"What about your cut?"

She grinned and patted the pockets on her tactical-style pants. "I'm good and now I'm square with that bitch."

Ah, she must have taken a handful of jewels, if he had to guess. Always easy money. He snorted softly. "I'll get it to the SUV."

She narrowed her gaze on him. "You're not on this job willingly either, are you?"

He shook his head.

That seemed to satisfy her, though it was hard to tell with her mask. "Hopefully I never see you again."

"Same. Be safe," he murmured.

She paused, then nodded and raced out of there.

He picked up the cylinder, grabbed a vase he recognized as quality on the way out, then reset the alarm before he strolled out the front door. After clicking the comm back on, he said, "On my way to you guys." As he stepped past the big security gate, peered out onto the street, a light from inside a vehicle flashed once.

Lyosha.

He sent off a quick text, then hurried to the waiting SUV.

Don, crouched in the very back, popped open the hatch.

Dimitri handed him the cylinder and the vase.

"Where's Ava?" he asked, looking behind Dimitri even as he snapped his laptop shut.

"Gone."

Don's eyes widened, then he shrugged.

"Make sure this gets to Irene. Tell her I'll be in contact."

"Come on," Eli called from the front. "We need to get out of here." The sound of his hand tapping against the steering wheel was audible.

Don simply tucked the vase under his arm and nodded.

Dimitri shut the hatch, then raced back to Lyosha's waiting SUV, jumped in the back seat. He was surprised Viktor was in the vehicle. "You didn't have to come," he said as he strapped in, pulled his mask off.

"You used to be one of my people." Viktor shrugged. "And now you're my friend."

He wasn't sure why but the words settled inside him. "Thank you." He knew he was lucky to have people to count on, people to call when he was in trouble.

"What happened to the other one?" Lyosha asked as he pulled away from the curb smoothly. "The female."

"Gone. Didn't seem to trust Irene either." And Dimitri thought that was probably smart on her part.

"Now that that's done, we're going to handle Irene." Viktor's voice was hard, like the man who'd once been feared among Miami's criminal element. Hell, he still was.

"Good. How's Zamira?" he asked.

"With Mila at my place. Worried, but safe."

He knew she'd be worried, but her safety was the priority. He laid his head back, shoved out a sigh. This mess was almost over.

After tomorrow morning, his life should go back to normal—

ish. Because he didn't want exactly what he'd had before, he wanted a life with Zamira in it.

But he needed to make sure that she really wanted him, that once the intensity of the situation wore off, things between them were real.

CHAPTER TWENTY-ONE

Zamira shifted as the bed dipped, then sat straight up, her eyes bleary. "I tried to stay awake." She reached for Dimitri, shoving the covers out of the way.

"It's fine, trust me." He pulled her into a hug and buried his face against her neck. "It's over. Mostly."

She squeezed him tight, breathed in his familiar scent. "Mostly?"

Sighing, he leaned back. "The job is done and we got away clean, but I've got a meeting tomorrow morning. *Then* it should be over."

"What kind of meeting?"

He paused, watched her with those dark blue, soulful eyes. She'd fallen asleep with the lamp on in Mila's guest room, so she could see him clearly.

"You don't want to tell me?" she asked quietly.

"Not really."

"I was married to a man who kept me in the dark about a lot of things." She knew they weren't married, not even close, but she still expected a certain level of openness. Especially after everything they'd been through together.

"I'm meeting with Irene. With some other interested parties."

"Other interested parties? Like maybe Lyosha and probably Lizzy Caldwell?"

He gave a small smile. "I don't think Lizzy will be there, but her husband will be."

Zamira's eyes widened. "Oh." She knew of the Caldwell family. Of course she did, considering she lived in Miami. Her brother-in-law worked for them and now Angel was close with Lizzy—a woman who Zamira genuinely liked.

"Tomorrow should effectively sever any issue I have with Irene and any issue you have with Ryba. If she doesn't back off…" He paused. "She's going to, unless she's completely stupid.

And she's not."

Zamira wanted to ask more questions, but Dimitri looked positively exhausted. "Okay, good. You want to get some sleep?"

He stripped his T-shirt off and stood. "You go back to sleep. I'm going to grab a shower first. Want to wash off the night."

She watched as he stepped into the connected bathroom, then when she heard the water running, she stripped off her short pajama set. From where she was, she heard him let out a low groan.

Not a sexual one, one of pure exhaustion.

She moved the shower curtain, stepped inside with him and hugged him from behind, laying her head on his back.

He held on to her arms with his own as the water beat down over them.

"Want to talk about tonight?"

"Everything went smoothly," he finally said. "Just so easy, even though we barely had any time to prep. At one time I would have loved a job like that. But the whole time all I could think about was you. Losing you."

She held him tighter. "I'm so sorry you had to do this job at all." He'd been dragged back into a world he'd left because of her past.

"It's not that. I just…" He turned, pulled her with him under the pulsing water. "I don't want to lose you, that's all."

"You're not going to lose me." She wasn't sure why he was saying that, what had brought it on. She wasn't even sure what they were, relationship wise, but she knew that she wanted him in her life, wanted to eventually introduce her children to him. He was the kind of man who showed up when he said he would, who protected those he cared for with a rabid fierceness.

"You're amazing," he finally said into the quiet.

"You're pretty amazing yourself." She leaned back slightly, though kept her breasts pressed to his chest, enjoying the skin-to-skin contact.

He cupped her cheek. "I'm just worried you're going to regret getting tangled up with me."

The raw vulnerability in his voice tore at her. "Not possible." She slid her hands down his back, clutching onto his ass tight. She wouldn't be able to convince him with words, but she was going to show him exactly how much he meant to her.

He was already hard, his thick erection heavy against her abdomen, but the moment she tugged him close he crushed his mouth over hers.

It was as if he'd been waiting for her to make the first move.

He pinned her against the tile wall as she grabbed onto his shoulders, lifted one leg up, wrapping it around him, spreading herself for him.

Reaching between their bodies, he cupped her mound, started teasing his finger along her folds as he continued kissing her.

She nipped and bit his bottom lip, feeling consumed with the need to have him inside her. And not because she'd been making up for lost time, but because this was Dimitri.

A man she'd completely fallen for. She didn't even know how to tell him. This was so new and foreign to her. It had been so long since she'd been with anyone and she'd never felt about anyone like she did for Dimitri.

He was that one in a million. The man who could break her heart if he wanted to. And yeah, she knew it was too soon for the L word, but…she knew how she felt.

When he slid a finger inside her, she jerked against him, her body sensitive and primed.

"Foreplay later," she ordered before biting his bottom lip again. She felt too desperate right now, didn't want the buildup but the payoff instead.

He let out a low laugh, the rumble reverberating through her. God, she loved when he laughed or smiled, showed that softer side of himself.

He grabbed her hips, lifted her up so she was pinned between the wall and his rock-hard body, and slid inside her in a slow, steady thrust.

She arched her back against the wall, her breasts rubbing against his chest as he thrust deep. There was so much she wanted to say to him but she couldn't find the words. So she rolled her hips against his, taking him as deep as he could go.

They found a rhythm quickly, the water beating down around them as they joined their bodies over and over.

In that moment she was consumed with him, the rest of the world blocked out as he completely filled her. It was like they'd always been together, been connected.

She slid a hand up his chest, her fingers memorizing the feel of him even as he reached between their bodies, ran his thumb over her pulsing clit. The stimulation had her jerking against him, her inner walls tightening faster and faster.

The more he teased her, the quicker her climax built until her orgasm surged through her. He'd learned her body so quickly, learned exactly what she liked, how hard she liked it.

He grabbed onto her hips tight then, releasing his own climax with a growl as he thrust until they were both breathing erratically but barely moving.

She slowly let her legs fall from him, her knees a little shaky as her feet met the tile.

He held her up, buried his face against her neck again and just embraced her for a long time as the water continued to fall around them.

She wanted to tell him that she'd fallen for him, that she was pretty sure she was in love with him, but...they'd been on one date. Then they'd been trapped under the same roof because of her. She didn't want to freak him out even as the word "love" rolled around in her head.

Because...she did love him. All of him.

She just wasn't sure if they would survive the real world.

CHAPTER TWENTY-TWO

Energy buzzed through Dimitri as he stepped into the restaurant with Viktor and Lyosha. It was a small diner, one Irene owned and frequented.

The place was quaint and the prices were low. It surprised him that Irene owned the place, let alone ate here frequently, because it was basically a dive—with incredible food. But he knew she'd come from nothing, had clawed her way to where she was now. If he had to guess, the place had sentimental value to her.

Lyosha went to the countertop and ordered a coffee while Dimitri stayed with Viktor, striding right up to Irene's booth.

Two men stepped in front of them to intervene, but Irene simply said, "They're fine." She eyed them curiously, her gaze lingering on Viktor for a long moment, clearly assessing him. "This is a surprise." Her tone was neutral as Viktor, then Dimitri slid in on the opposite side of the red Naugahyde booth.

"It shouldn't be. You thought you could take one of my people for a job and not run it by me? Not ask for permission?" Viktor's voice was low, even, and for anyone who knew him, that was a bad thing.

Irene flicked a glance at Dimitri, then looked back at Viktor.

She was in a pale pink Chanel suit, a strand of pearls around her slim neck. And the pulse in her neck kicked up. "You left the business long ago. It was my understanding he was a free agent."

Viktor was silent for a long moment, those ice-blue eyes staring at her with pure anger. He wasn't hiding who he was today. Gone was the man who'd picked up his daughter this morning and kissed her little tummy until she dissolved into giggles. This was the man Dimitri had known long ago. And he was pissed. "Dimitri will always be one of my people, and if you think I've gone anywhere, you're stupid. And I know you're not stupid. Which leaves me with only one conclusion."

Irene cleared her throat. "If you're looking for his cut—"

"Be. Quiet." Viktor's voice was so low now it was a rumble in his throat.

Irene's two men stepped forward slightly, pushing off the countertop where they'd been lounging in front of their coffees. She held up a hand, stilled them.

"I don't want a cut. I don't want anything from you—except that you leave my people alone. Dimitri is one of mine and he always will be. If anything happens to him, or anyone he cares about, you're the first person I'll come for. If anything happens at one of his businesses, the same applies. If your nephew does something stupid, you will be held responsible for his actions."

"This is just a misunderstanding," Irene murmured. Her expression and tone were neutral, but there was fear in her eyes. She couldn't hide it.

"I don't think it is. And I know it wasn't a misunderstanding when your nephew pulled a weapon on Lizzy Caldwell."

Irene went very still at that, her nostrils flaring. "What?"

Viktor's mouth curved up, all predator now. "He didn't tell you?" He jerked a thumb behind him to the opposite side of the diner. "Her husband Porter is over there with his brothers. Their father is waiting in the parking lot."

Irene cleared her throat once, twice, and for the first time since Dimitri had known her, she looked unsure of herself. She licked her lips, an out of character nervous action. "I was not aware of this. When did it happen? And is Mrs. Caldwell okay?"

"She's unharmed. Which is the only reason your nephew is still breathing."

Irene glanced around him and Viktor, paled when she saw Viktor had spoken the truth about those sitting across the diner. Yeah, she didn't want to make enemies of the Caldwell family. They were powerful, had reach well beyond Miami. "What do you want from me?" she finally asked, straightening in her seat. She might be worried now, but she was hiding it well enough.

"To stay away from my people." Viktor squeezed Dimitri's shoulder once. "From anyone who has any connections to Red Stone Security. And to make sure your nephew never steps foot in this city again. If I get a whiff—"

"He won't." Her words were whiplash sharp. "He will not be a problem for you," she said, looking at Dimitri. "Or anyone in your life. He will never return to Miami. You have my word. I will personally take care of him, and if there are amends to make, I will make them." She flicked a glance behind them again.

"If you need to, I'm sure the Caldwells will reach out. As far as I'm concerned, we're good if you keep your family in line and stay away from me and mine."

Irene held out her hand, shook Viktor's once, then nodded politely at Dimitri.

Dimitri nodded back, then said, "The woman from the job last night?" He didn't even know her real name, but he'd liked her.

"What about her?"

"She's off-limits now too. Stay away from her."

Irene gritted her teeth, very much looked like she wanted to argue, but finally nodded. "Done."

Dimitri slid out of the booth, made his way to the glass door with Viktor and Lyosha. The Caldwells dropped a few bills on their own table, then stood and left as well. Though Porter lingered, eyed Irene for a very long moment. No one in the place said a word as they all cleared out.

Dimitri didn't talk again until he was in Viktor's SUV. "That went well."

Viktor turned to look at him from the front passenger seat as Lyosha steered out of the parking lot. "It did. Who was the woman from last night?"

Dimitri lifted a shoulder. "I don't know." But she clearly hadn't been a fan of Irene's, so that counted for something. And he'd wanted to piss off Irene just a little more. She deserved it for all the trouble she'd caused him.

Viktor grinned, shook his head, then turned back around.

"You can just take me home," Dimitri said from the back as he pulled his cell phone out.

"Zamira is still at my place with Mila though." Lyosha's frown was visible in the rearview mirror.

"I know. I'll call her once I'm home. I'm going to give her some space. She was thrown into a volatile situation and had to depend on me to help her. I think she needs space. She's been through a lot." Far too much. He wanted to be with her more than anything, but this was necessary for her. And he needed to make sure she wanted him for him, not just the security he'd offered. And she needed to be able to choose with a clear head. Not have him pressuring her, even unintentionally.

Lyosha grunted his disapproval.

Well, too bad. He didn't understand.

"Space is a mistake," Viktor said.

"Respectfully, I know what I'm doing." And he wasn't asking for permission.

Viktor snorted softly. "I think you *believe* that you do."

Ignoring him, Dimitri texted Zamira. *All is good. You'll be able to go home soon.* He wanted her to know that she was finally safe, that she didn't have to worry about that bastard Ryba anymore.

Because Dimitri had no doubt Irene would be taking care of Ryba herself.

~

"Are you...done with me?" Holding her phone up to her ear, Zamira spoke to Dimitri as she sat on the edge of the guest bed, unable to believe that he hadn't come back this morning. She'd thought he'd texted her because he didn't want to talk in front of Lyosha, but then Lyosha had come back to his and Mila's place.

Alone.

"No, no! I...knew if I came back to Lyosha and Mila's I'd be selfish, that I'd take you back to my place and we wouldn't leave my bed for the next week."

"Is that supposed to be a bad thing?" A week in bed with him sounded like heaven.

"I don't want you to feel beholden to me or pressured to be with me. You had no choice before—"

"Uh, I had a choice whether I wanted to sleep with you or not. And I very much did." Soooo much. She wanted him here right now so she could do it some more. "Is this...because I have kids?" God, she should have known. Maybe the reality of her being a single mom was settling in and now he was simply done.

"What? No! I mean, I know nothing about kids, but no. I just want to make sure that you're sure you want to be with me, with no pressure and with space from me."

She took a deep breath. *Space? Bullshit.* "Do you want to be with me?" She needed a straight answer.

"More than anything." There was such longing in his voice, it sliced right through her.

She bit back a groan at the mixed signals. She thought about pushing him, but wasn't sure that was the right move, wasn't sure of *anything*. When Lyosha had returned without Dimitri an hour ago... She was still reeling from the sense of loss and confusion. "So, you just want me to, what, *think* about us?"

"Yes."

She gritted her teeth, but reined in her frustration. "I don't need time to think, Dimitri."

He paused, then said, "I think you do."

"Okay," she finally said. "When I call you later, are you going to answer?" She was so far out of this dating game that she wasn't sure if this was his polite way of trying to ghost her. Was this how people broke up with each other now? With hollow promises? She didn't think so, but she'd heard a lot of horror stories from her friends.

"Of course."

"Okay, then. I'll talk to you soon."

Once they disconnected, she tossed her phone down and headed to find her sister—who was still drinking coffee in her pajamas in the kitchen.

Mila looked up from her tablet and smiled. "Hey...oh, what's up?"

Stupid tears pricked her eyes but she batted them away. "I don't know! I think Dimitri just broke up with me." Or maybe he hadn't. Everything was a mess.

"What?" Mila jumped off the stool, tugged her into her arms.

Zamira didn't care about her tears now as she buried her face in her sister's shoulder. She was the one who always comforted her kids, but now...she was off-kilter in a way she hadn't felt in forever. "I don't think I'm cut out for dating," she finally murmured, lifting her head. "He said a bunch of crap about how he still wants me but that I need to think about what I want." Or whatever. "It sounds like a bunch of lies. I told him I didn't need time to think—I want to be with him." She cared for him so much her chest ached with it. He'd barreled right into her life and stepped up to protect her when he hadn't had to.

"Dimitri is being a dumbass," Lyosha said as he stepped into the room, dressed in slacks and a button-down.

"I'll say," growled Mila.

"He does *not* want to break up with you either," Lyosha continued.

Hope twisted hard in her chest. "Really?"

"Yes, really. Just trust me on this. He will come to his senses."

Zamira swiped away the last of her tears as she tried to wrap her mind around the vast change in Dimitri. Just hours ago in the early morning hours they'd made love. Now...he wanted to give her space? *Ugh.* More like he wanted space for himself.

His reasoning sounded like an out for him. "Am I okay to go home?" she asked Lyosha. She figured she was since Clarita, Carlos and their kids had already gone home but she wanted to confirm.

He nodded once, but added, "Yes, but you are welcome to stay here as long as you like."

"Yes," Mila added. "Please stay."

"No, I'm fine. But thank you both for your hospitality. I'm sure you want your place back." And she wanted to be alone right now, wanted to wallow in self-pity.

Lyosha simply shrugged, and before Mila could answer, their white and orange cat Nala raced in chasing their border collie Boots. His nails clicked on the floor as he ran right at Lyosha, jumping up at him.

Lyosha snickered as he scooped up Boots—who promptly started licking him like crazy. "Is Nala picking on you?" he murmured, his tone indulgent.

Mila simply shook her head, but it was clear she was fighting a laugh. "He's such a baby sometimes."

Zamira laughed, watching as Nala wound her way around Mila's legs until she was picked up as well. Taking a step back, she said, "I'm going to grab my stuff." She'd never unpacked, just took out the basics, and the truth was she wanted to be home.

Wanted to be around all her things—her kids' things. As soon as she got home, she was going to start a video chat with them.

Then…she wasn't sure if she should call Dimitri again or wait for him to reach out, or what. He'd thrown her for such a loop.

No, she wouldn't call him. She had her life back, some down-time. She'd hoped to enjoy a lot of that time with him, but she wasn't going to spend the rest of her free time moping around.

Well, maybe a little.

She'd already made up her mind about him, about them—she wanted to be with him. And it sounded like he was the one who needed to make up his mind.

He needed to figure out what he wanted. Maybe now that he had *space*, he'd figure it out.

CHAPTER TWENTY-THREE

"I don't know if I'm scared or impressed." Porter leaned against the window in the high-rise condo he and Lizzy kept downtown as he looked out at the bright day. Their actual home was in a quiet suburb with their three kids, but this place was close to work. And if they decided to go to an event downtown or near the beach, often the whole family crashed here instead of driving home if it was late.

"By what?"

"You."

She snorted softly and the little clicking from her keyboard was the only sound for a long moment. "I'm pretty sure you're both scared and impressed by me."

"I did marry a terrifying woman." Sometimes it was still hard to wrap his mind around that he'd found her, that she'd agreed to marry him. Lizzy was in a class all her own and he was so damn grateful for the life they'd created, the kids they had. When he'd learned that Ryba had pulled a gun on Angel—with Lizzy in the same building—he'd lost years of his life. She was the heart of their family and he couldn't imagine a life without her.

"True fact." She let out a victorious sound he recognized well. His wife was on the hunt and she was about to destroy her prey.

"Should I ask?"

She stretched out on the couch, pushed her laptop to the side and crossed one black-and-white sneaker over the other. Her shoes were covered in manga characters—a Mother's Day gift from their oldest son who was currently into it.

Porter had learned the most random things over the last decade, from Minecraft to manga, thanks to his kids.

"She's going down." And Lizzy was clearly satisfied with whatever she'd just done or found online.

The "she" referred to Irene Gorcyca. Porter had wanted to go after her and her organization directly, but thankfully his wife's level head had prevailed. As usual. "How?"

"It's shockingly simple. I hacked into CCTV cameras and followed that van from last night. I think I found one of Irene's stash houses. If so...the Feds might be able to RICO her. Just depends on if they can make a racketeering charge stick. Either way, she's going to have to answer for a lot of crimes."

Gorcyca was so dirty, Porter was hopeful it would. "And it'll never fall back on any of us."

"Nope." Lizzy jumped up and smoothed down her *word nerd* T-shirt. "No one will even know the information came from me. It won't ever be in any random FBI files. The Feds will think they got the info from another law enforcement agency. And that agency won't have any record of sending it. Magic, baby."

He blinked once and shoved off the window as he stalked to his wife. "Do I even want to know how you did that?" It was ridiculously hot when she went all rogue hacker. He didn't understand half of the stuff she did, but he sure as hell appreciated it.

"Pretty sure you know the answer to that," she murmured, her gaze falling to his mouth as he reached her.

He grasped onto her hips, tugged her close—just as the doorbell rang.

She laughed lightly as he scowled, and stepped back. "Be *nice*," she whispered, even though the people ringing the bell couldn't possibly hear.

"I will." He would be nice, *for now*.

A moment later he heard the door open, then his wife let out a squeal. Then a male voice, followed by a soft female voice.

Porter had to force himself to smile as Lizzy entered with her brother Benny and his fiancée, Chrissy. He wasn't one to hold a grudge, but Benny had put Lizzy's life in danger, more than once. Sure, he'd been an addict—drinking, gambling, drugs, you name it —but it didn't excuse any of it. Not to Porter.

"Porter." Benny stepped forward, looking far different than the last time he'd seen him all those years ago. He'd filled out, had a healthy bronze glow, his hair was a little longer, around his shoulders now. He looked...healthy, happy.

"Benny, good to see you." Not really, but he would pretend to make Lizzy happy.

Benny grinned. "I almost believe you," he said with a laugh, holding out a hand.

Porter took it with a snort.

Lizzy smacked his shoulder. "Porter *is* happy to see you. And we're both happy to meet Chrissy." She turned to her sister-in-law to-be, her smile wide. His wife was practically bursting with joy right now.

The redhead was petite with big eyes, but her smile matched Lizzy's.

And when Benny looked back at his soon-to-be wife, pulled her close to him, it was clear to see that he loved her. This was not the same addict who'd gone into WITSEC years ago. No, this was a man who'd done the work and been allowed to start over, to make better choices.

People deserve second chances, Dad! He could hear his son Maddox's voice in his head. "It's definitely a pleasure to meet you," he said, holding his hand out to the woman. "And I know you guys have a rental, but we've got the space if you want to stay with us."

Behind them, Lizzy's mouth fell open. She hadn't asked once if Benny could stay with them, probably because she'd known he'd be grumpy about it. Because his wife was damn amazing, and while he never forgot that, he should have offered before now.

"Oh…ah." Benny looked at Chrissy, who just shrugged. Then he looked back at Porter. "We've got our dog, so—"

"We've got one too. A friendly Lab. But if you think your dog won't get along with ours, it's not a big deal. I just wanted to throw the offer out there."

"We'd love to." Benny smiled at him. "We haven't even unpacked or anything. Thank you."

"No problem." He should have offered long ago, was kicking himself for not doing it sooner, especially seeing the expression on Lizzy's face right now.

"I'd say this calls for a celebration. Let's go grab your stuff," Lizzy said. "Then we'll have a big barbeque at our place tonight. Unless that's too overwhelming?"

"No way. I want to meet my nephews." Benny's whole face lit up as he spoke.

"Good, it's settled, then. Let me grab my stuff and we'll meet you guys in the lobby and follow you to your rental?"

Benny and Chrissy nodded, and the moment the front door shut behind them Lizzy threw her arms around Porter.

She kissed him hard, wrapping her legs around him tightly, making him stumble, then laugh.

"You can't get me all worked up now," he growled against her mouth.

"Thank you for asking him to stay. It means so much to me and to him. Now he knows you've truly forgiven him."

"I should have done it before now." He knew how much Benny meant to her, and he should have put aside his own shit a lot earlier.

"It doesn't matter." She let her legs fall, but kept her arms wrapped tight around him. "The fact that you're inviting him over means everything to me. Thank you."

"You don't need to thank me. He's your family." And it was clear he'd turned over a new leaf. "And it'll be good for him to get to know the boys."

She buried her face against his chest, her dark curls escaping from her braid. "I love you even more."

"I love you more every day." He wasn't even sure how it was possible, but every moment with her, even the ones where she made him crazy, was better than all the time he spent away from her.

His world was infinitely brighter with her in it. Hell, the world itself was brighter with her in it. Which was why his instinct had always been to neutralize any threat against her, "caveman style" as she liked to say.

Including Ryba. So if Gorcyca didn't take care of her nephew, Porter would.

CHAPTER TWENTY-FOUR

Zamira stared at her phone as Dimitri's name flashed on the screen. She'd come home, showered, called her kids. Twice. Then had a glass of wine and had ordered Thai delivery.

All while obsessing over Dimitri, wondering what the heck had gone wrong between them. Why he hadn't been able to take her at her word that she didn't need any space, that she knew her own mind enough to know that she wanted him.

"Hey," she answered on the fourth ring.

He shoved out a sigh of what sounded a lot like relief. "Hey, how are you?"

"Good." Not good. She wanted answers. Wanted to know exactly where they stood.

"Good."

Silence stretched between them, beyond awkward. At the sound of the doorbell, she pushed up from the couch and headed through the kitchen toward the front of the house. "So...how are you?"

"Good. Look, I'm sorry about before. Are you free tonight?"

She wanted to say no, but she was pretty weak where Dimitri was concerned, and a wave of relief hit her that he wanted to see her so soon. "I just ordered Thai food and there's enough for two." Okay, there was enough for a soccer team, but she wasn't going to tell him that she'd planned to drown her sadness in food tonight. "Do you want to come over?" she asked as she opened the door. But she froze as she found Kurt Ryba on her doorstep, bags of food in hand. "Oh my God."

He dropped the bags and grabbed her phone from her hand, smashed it to the ground even as he shoved her back into the foyer.

Before she could think or blink, he had a gun shoved in her face, his expression set. Terrifying. "I want the password to a bank account. It's my only access to an offshore account. Without it, I can't get my funds."

Her heart was racing out of control as she tried to process his words. Panic punched through her, sweat pricking the bottom of her spine as she tried not to stare at the gun. "And you think I have it?" she whispered.

"No, but your husband had it saved somewhere." He cursed, looked past her. "Is your boyfriend here?"

"No. We...broke up. Oh my God, did you hurt the delivery driver?" Another surge of panic spiraled through her.

"What? No. I just gave him a fifty when he drove up and said I'd bring it inside. Now where would Lucas have kept a password?" He motioned with his gun that she should move farther into the house.

She did, walking backward, staring at the terrifying weapon. "I..." She didn't know. She didn't *know*!

He pressed the gun to her temple and a flash of ice slicked down her spine.

She was going to die. He was going to kill her right where she stood if she screwed up. *No!* She would be smart... "I can't think when you're holding a gun on me," she finally got out, her voice raspy.

He lowered it halfway so that it wasn't directly in her face and she sucked in air, able to actually take a full breath again. "Think hard," he said, his tone threatening.

"Okay. I...I'm trying to think. I donated most of his clothes and you looked through everything... Wait, he has yearbooks up in the attic! Maybe it's in there. I keep them stored with the Christmas decorations. I forgot about them, but I don't know. Maybe he kept what you're looking for there?"

"You'd better hope so," he snarled. "And you'd better not be lying."

She held up her hands, couldn't stop the tremble that snaked through her at the promise of death in his eyes. "I have no reason to lie. I don't want anything from you or from him." Other than for Ryba to get out of her life and leave her the hell alone.

He eyed her for another long moment, then looked around the interior of her foyer and into the dining room right off it. "How do you get into your attic?"

"This way." She motioned down the hall, wondering if Dimitri had tried to call her back. Or hopefully called the cops. Something. "There's an opening right in the hallway to the bedrooms." There was also one in the garage and she just hoped she'd be able to get away from him long enough to use it to escape. Her attic was huge and escaping out one of the openings was her only chance.

Because she had no doubt Ryba was going to kill her, whether he found what he was looking for or not. She couldn't depend on Dimitri calling in backup or getting here in time. She was going to save herself—her kids were *not* losing both their parents.

When they stood under the square inlaid panel, she nodded at it. "I can't reach the door without a step stool. There's one in the kitchen."

"Move back," he ordered, then reached up, but it was too high even for him and he was over six feet tall. "All right, come on."

They headed to the kitchen where she indicated he should grab the stool out of the pantry. And he kept his gun on her the entire time. He also made sure she wasn't close enough to rush him.

Not that she was going to, but it was clear he was being cautious.

Her heart was a staccato beat in her chest and she could only hope an opportunity to escape would present itself. She also hoped Dimitri had called the police or something. Though she had a feeling he would show up.

And that scared her as much as it gave her hope. He was deadly and capable, but Ryba had a gun and was on edge. So much could go wrong so quickly. Fear squeezed her throat; regret made it worse.

"What is it?" Ryba asked as they stopped under the panel.

"Just thinking that my kids are going to grow up without both their parents when you kill me." Maybe he had a heart hiding in that hollow chest, would feel a little guilt and second-guess killing her. She'd try anything at this point.

"I'm not going to kill you," he snarled.

But she didn't believe him.

"If you help me find what I'm looking for, I have no need to hurt you," he said as he climbed the ladder. "I just want what's mine, and then I'm getting out of the country. That's it."

Yeah, right. She was a loose end and she knew it. But she didn't respond. She cleared her throat, stepped back as he pulled the rope. The panel opened and the stairs unfolded with a squeak. "Does your aunt know you're here?" she asked, thinking of what Dimitri had told her. *Please get here, Dimitri.*

Ryba snorted and motioned for her to climb up first. "She's got enough problems of her own. And soon I won't have to listen to anything that bitch says."

As she climbed up into the dusty space, she felt around for the switch on the nearest wall. As soon as she hit it, the dim bulb came on with a buzz, illuminating the dusty plastic bins stacked around the room.

The first stack was all Christmas and other holiday decorations, each one clearly labeled. Though the contents were visible. "Behind the Christmas stuff are a couple of bins of Lucas's stuff. Yearbooks, baseball cards, other random things." She had no clue if a password might be in there, but it was the only thing she could think of where he might have kept something. No one would ever look there—and she hadn't wanted to just toss his childhood things. She'd wanted her kids to be able to look at old pictures of their father.

"You should have brought them to the storage facility." Ryba's voice was a low growl as he stalked across the wood flooring toward the bins.

"I didn't think about this stuff."

He simply made a grunting sound and kicked one of the bins out of the way.

She winced at the sound of something breaking, but gritted her teeth. A few broken bulbs were nothing. He could break everything. She just wanted to escape. To *live*.

She looked down at the opening, knew she'd never make it down the stairs. He'd shoot her before she got onto the ladder, no problem. With the light streaming up from the hallway, she'd basically have a spotlight on her.

No.

She watched as he ripped off one of the tops and pulled out a yearbook with his free hand.

He paused, then looked at her. "Why don't you get your ass over here and make yourself useful?"

She forced a nod, and when he looked back down at the yearbook, started shaking it to see if anything fell out, she lunged back, flipped the light switch off. She might not be able to escape through that exit, but there was another way.

Another exit. But she'd have to crawl through her attic to get to it. And she'd have to do it in the dark, would have to blind him so she could escape.

And this was her only chance.

Little bits of light still shone from the hallway, but it was from below. She was completely hidden now as she inched backward, farther into the shadows.

"Turn it back on," he snapped. "You can't escape and I don't want to shoot you."

The word *yet* seemed to suspend in the air, unsaid but heard. She stayed quiet and took another step back.

Bang!

She jumped at the gunshot, dove to the ground as insulation splintered all around her. Heart racing, she stayed low and started crawling in the opposite direction, the darkness her friend.

Ryba snarled behind her and she knew she had a limited time before he found that light switch. Then it was game over.

"Fuck!" There was a crash behind her, then a clattering sound.

She crawled faster, her heart in her throat as she hurried across the wood beam. The attic floor wasn't completely finished so if he tried to follow her in the dark, he'd fall through the ceiling below. Hopefully break his legs.

Another thud sounded behind her, maybe him kicking another bin.

As she reached the opposite side of the attic, ignoring the cobwebs covering her face and hair, she reached around blindly for the other opening into her garage. One of the selling points of this house had been the huge attic and the possibility of turning it into an extra room. Right about now she was so damn grateful she'd never done that.

Her hand clasped around something raised. The folded ladder!

"Stupid bitch!" His angry words came out of the dark a moment before the light flared on.

She looked behind her, couldn't see him. Just stacks of bins in the way, a bit of dim yellow light shining behind them.

Focusing on the task, she ignored the sound of his boots stomping in her direction as she shoved the panel open.

Bang!

Wood splintered a foot from her. There was no time to release the ladder. She slid over the side of the opening, fell right onto the hood of her car.

Metal crunched under her, the painful impact of the fall jarring her whole body. Palms damp, she half slid, half fell off the hood and slammed her hand against the garage door opener.

As it started to lift up, she raced for the opening, not waiting for the door to get high enough. She dove under it as another gunshot exploded from the attic.

It pinged against metal this time but she shoved to her feet and ran.

Straight into a wall of muscle.

She bounced back, stumbled and looked up into Dimitri's face. "Ryba's in the attic with a gun!" she cried, torn between terror and relief.

"Run to my SUV!" He shoved her in the direction of the street then raced back into her garage as he pulled out his own weapon.

She wanted to run after him, to stop him, but knew that would be stupid. She would just distract him.

"Zamira?" Mrs. Shirley, her next-door neighbor, strolled across her lawn, cocktail in hand. "What's going on, dear? I thought I heard fireworks."

"Inside now. We need to call the cops." She grasped the older woman's arm and steered her straight back into her home. "An armed man broke into my house."

"Oh dear!" She patted her pocket, pulled out her phone and Zamira snapped it up, called 911 immediately.

Before they picked up, she heard a very loud gunshot. Her heart seized.

Dimitri.

CHAPTER TWENTY-FIVE

Dimitri knelt next to Kurt Ryba's prone body, checked his pulse for good measure. Given the odd angle he'd fallen from the attic opening and the bullet hole in his chest, he wasn't getting up ever again.

But Dimitri wanted to be sure.

Dead.

He tucked his weapon away and hurried out into the driveway, back to his SUV. When he saw it was empty, low-grade panic buzzed deep in his gut. What if Ryba had been working with someone?

Fuck—

"Dimitri!"

He turned at the sound of Zamira's voice, saw her running across her neighbor's lawn, wide-eyed, her hair wild around her face.

Immediately he scanned for another threat even as he hurried toward her. "Are you okay? Was he alone?"

She nodded even as tears rolled down her face. "It was just him. He wanted some bank password or something," she said on a sob, her voice breaking. "When I heard that gunshot, I thought…"

He pulled her to him, wrapped his arms around her. "He's gone and he can't hurt you again." The sound of sirens started to grow louder and he knew that within minutes this place was going to be a shitshow. "Listen," he murmured, gently rubbing up and down her spine. "We're going to have to give our statements and I'm definitely being brought down to the police station. They might even cuff me."

"What?" She stepped back, staring up at him. "Why?"

"I'm not saying they will cuff me, but I killed someone so it's a possibility." He spoke quickly, wanting to explain everything while they still had time. He was aware of some of her neighbors on their lawns now, watching, but all his focus was on her. "They will want full reports from us and they'll separate us while we give our stories. I'm going to call my lawyer and I think you need to call your sister Mila. Lyosha will come down to the station with her and if they don't let you out soon enough, he'll raise hell. Just tell the truth and everything will be okay. Okay?"

She nodded and batted tears away as a police car pulled up into her driveway.

Dimitri stepped back, pointed to the garage as two uniformed officers jumped out of their car. "The intruder is in there," he said, keeping his hands visible as he spoke. "And he's dead. I killed him in self-defense. My weapon, which I have a permit for, is on me. I'm keeping my hands up so you can retrieve it."

From that moment, everything moved at warp speed, and just as he'd known, Zamira was taken away in a separate vehicle.

At least they were being gentle with her. That was the only thing that made all this bearable.

Because all this was his fault. He never should have let her go, never should have insisted she get space from him.

It didn't matter that Gorcyca had said Ryba wouldn't be a problem. He should have made sure. Because of his oversight, he could have lost her forever.

He wasn't making that mistake again. If she forgave him, he wasn't letting her go.

CHAPTER TWENTY-SIX

Zamira jumped up as Dimitri strode out with Viktor and a man she didn't recognize. But if she had to guess, he was Dimitri's lawyer. He spoke quietly to Dimitri, then Viktor, then left, already talking on his phone as he strode out of the police station waiting room.

Even though Dimitri had told her to call her family, she'd opted not to. She'd answered all the police's questions, and her house—the crime scene—backed up her story. The truth. If they'd tried to arrest her, she'd have called, but now she was glad she hadn't.

She only had so much mental bandwidth at the moment.

"You're good to go?" she asked as Dimitri and Viktor approached. She didn't know Viktor well, but really liked his wife and kids.

"Free to go with no follow-up. With both our accounts and the copies of the video from your camera system, there's going to be no problem." He swept his gaze over her, as if looking for injuries. "You're sure you're okay? They said you didn't want to go to the hospital."

"I'm fine. Sore from jumping on the hood of my car, but fine."

No broken bones at least. But she winced as she thought about all the damage at her house as well as her vehicle.

"Worry about calling insurance in the morning," Viktor said to her as if he'd read her mind. "I'm going to take you back to your house so Dimitri can grab his car, then I suggest you go to his place and the two of you get some sleep."

She blinked at the other man, surprised by how many words he'd said at once. Zamira then looked at Dimitri, wondering if that was what he wanted.

"Sounds good to me," he murmured, falling in step with her as they headed out of the police station.

A wave of humidity rolled over her as they stepped outside, the promise of Florida summer close by. She pulled a hairband out of her purse and started braiding her hair as they reached Viktor's fancy SUV.

Dimitri opened the passenger door for her, but she shook her head. "I'll sit with you."

Once they were in the back seat together, she laid her head on his shoulder after she strapped in. And promptly fell asleep.

"WE'RE HERE?" Zamira rasped out, blinking as she looked around. Everything looked foreign, even her house with the crime scene tape still across her garage door.

"Yeah." Dimitri's voice was low, soothing. "Let's go pack a small bag, then you can sleep on the way to my place."

She wasn't even sure what time it was now, almost midnight, she realized when she saw the time on the dash. "Ah, okay. Thank you for driving us," she said as she slid out.

Viktor might have responded. She wasn't sure as she headed up her driveway.

Her neighborhood was quiet, but there were more traces of what had happened. Tire indentations from one of the cop cars that'd zoomed up were visible in the grass by her driveway. And of course the remnants of the crime scene tape. "We can go in?" she asked as Dimitri stepped up next to her.

"Yeah, they've done everything they need to."

"Is there…blood in my garage?"

"Yeah. I'll pay to have it cleaned. You won't have to ever look at it."

She wanted to tell him she'd take care of it herself, but felt almost numb as she stared at her two-story home, as she thought about how close she'd come to dying. To leaving her kids behind with no parents. To losing Dimitri. Tonight could have ended in her worst nightmare. "Thank you," she rasped out, because that was all she trusted herself to say.

It didn't take long to grab what she needed, and then they were once again driving. Miami was quiet this time of night, at least in the more suburban areas. There wasn't much traffic anywhere and they seemed to get all the green lights as Dimitri smoothly drove through the city.

"So what happened with the police? With…Ryba?" She knew he'd shot him, but she just… Maybe she wasn't sure what she was asking. She felt so out of sorts, untethered at the moment.

"He had a weapon and was going to shoot me so that part is open and closed. I've got a permit for my weapon so no issue there. Combined with him stalking you, harassing you, and his record, this is very open-and-shut for the cops."

That was good at least. "I have no idea if Lucas even had what he was looking for, that password. Would the bank account even be good now?"

"Some offshore accounts are like that. And if it's just been sitting there, unless someone else has access there's no reason it's not still there."

"I wish I didn't even know about it." She closed her eyes, let her head fall back.

"You never have to think about it again if you don't want."

"I don't want to think about him ever again." She shoved out a sigh. "But I'll have to because I've got to get my house patched up in the places he shot and—"

"I'll take care of all that."

"No. I'll do it. I've been handling my own life for a long time."

"I know. But I'd like to help. I know your kids come back soon and I know some guys who will put a rush on getting your house back together. Including cleaning the garage floor."

"I...don't know if I'm comfortable with you taking over like that. Not when you sort of ghosted me," she whispered, all her emotions from earlier rushing to the surface. She was walking a tightrope of emotions after the last few days.

"I'm sorry," he said as he pulled into his driveway, his gate closing behind them. "More than you know. I was...scared," he finally said.

"Of what?"

He turned to face her as he put his SUV in park in the garage. The sound of the garage door closing behind them was the only noise for a long moment as he watched her. "Of you, me, us."

She raised an eyebrow.

"I see a real future with you and I panicked. Acted like a dumbass."

She let out a startled laugh. "I won't argue with you there."

He gave her a small smile, reached across the center console and took her hand in his.

She laced her fingers through his, needing that connection. "So are you still scared?"

"Terrified that I'll screw up and drive you away."

"You've been protective and a little bossy and simply wonderful since I met you. And I'm still here. I'm so thankful for everything you've done. You saved my life." She swallowed back the onslaught of tears that wanted to rush up, somehow keeping them at bay.

"And I'd do it again in a heartbeat. I'm good with that kind of stuff. I'm just worried about the day-to-day stuff, your kids, everything." He sounded so vulnerable. Hell, looked vulnerable in that moment in a way she'd never seen from him before.

She brought his hand to her mouth, kissed his knuckles. "I'm a little worried about that stuff too. I wasn't sure we'd fit into your life. You're so organized, and my kids and I...we can be loud and messy."

He grinned, his expression softening. "I like loud and messy."

"Yeah, well, I like you."

"I love you," he blurted.

Her mouth fell open slightly at his words but... "I love you too." So much that it scared her.

Now he looked surprised by her confession. "You don't have to—"

"To what, say the truth? I *do* love you. I just thought it might freak you out if I told you so soon."

Now he was full-on grinning, looking ten years younger in that moment. "Never."

Leaning forward, she took his face in her hands, savoring the fact that he was here, that she could touch him. She could have lost him tonight and that terrified her on a whole other level.

He claimed her mouth and she kissed him right back.

She wasn't going to hold anything back from him, not after tonight. They'd been given a chance and she was going to grab it with both hands.

CHAPTER TWENTY-SEVEN

Two months later

Zamira stepped into the living room, surprised to find all the men from the party—and Lizzy—staring at the big-screen TV on Lyosha and Mila's wall.

Dimitri turned to glance at her, smiled sheepishly. "Sorry," he murmured, handing her the drink he'd promised to get her. "Got distracted."

She slid up to him, wrapped her arm around his middle and nodded at the screen. "What's going on?" They were at Lyosha and Mila's for a big summer party and all her family was there, a bunch of people from Mila's work, people Lyosha knew, and tons of kids. It was a madhouse out by the pool. Thankfully they had the space.

"Irene Gorcyca has been arrested."

"Took them long enough," Lizzy grumbled without turning around. The lean mom of three—and apparently a very skilled hacker—had her arms crossed over her chest, her body language clearly annoyed even from behind. "They should have had her in jail a month ago."

"They had to build a case," Porter murmured in a way that said they'd had this conversation before.

"They're bringing up the death of Ryba," Dimitri murmured, pulling Zamira back from the group, who had started collectively talking about the "slow-ass" legal system.

She winced, hating that she'd had a few seconds of "fame" months ago. The news had covered his death for a few days, but thankfully the coverage had been short and local. There was always so much crazy going on in Florida that it hadn't been much of a blip on anyone's radar. But it had been enough that she hated being on the news at all. She liked her privacy. At least it hadn't affected her kids.

She'd told them about it when they'd returned because she hadn't wanted to risk them hearing the news from someone else. They'd had questions and she'd answered as well as she could. To her surprise, they'd barely cared at all. They'd been way more interested in Dimitri, peppering her with all sorts of questions about him. So far, they really, really seemed to like him. She hadn't gotten the pushback she'd been bracing for.

"What are they saying about him?"

"Just mentioning that he was killed, was her nephew, and making a few random speculations. Wondering if she ordered him to break into your house."

"Oh my God," she muttered as they stepped into the kitchen. She sat at the island, took a sip of her water as Juan and Angel piled food onto their plates.

"What's going on?" Angel asked, adding another cupcake.

"Nothing, but I'm glad to see you got your appetite back."

Angel had been sick for months, barely able to keep anything down. She'd actually lost weight and now she was clearly making up for it.

"Me too. I feel like I could eat everything."

"You eat whatever you want, mi amore." Juan kissed her cheek before he snagged a cube of cheese from her plate.

"Then stop stealing my food," she grumbled as they headed back out to the pool.

Zamira snickered. "They're ridiculous."

"No kidding." Dimitri sat next to her, casually tossed his arm around the back of her chair. "It sounds like Gorcyca is going to have her hands full for years."

"You think they'll make the charges stick?"

"Oh yeah. Lizzy's annoyed it took so long, but they had to build a strong case. Lyosha told me that some of the charges won't last, but all the money laundering and drugs... She'll be going to jail for a very long time. She'll probably die in jail, considering her age."

"Wow."

Dimitri lifted a shoulder. "She's hurt a lot of people over the years."

Zamira nodded because it was true. A lot of Irene's crimes had come to light over the last month. Though they'd never been able to find out more about that bank account Ryba had wanted access to. Or Lucas's link to it. It was one of those things she'd had to put out of her mind because she didn't think she'd ever know if it still existed, or how much was in it if it did. Before she could respond, Andres hurried in, dripping water. "You're supposed to dry off, my love. Someone could slip and get hurt. And I'm sure Tia Mila doesn't appreciate you getting water everywhere."

"I'm sorry, Mama." But he didn't look sorry at all. "But I need to talk to Dimitri, man to man."

"Ah." Dimitri gave her a quick kiss, then slid off the stool, headed back outside with Andres.

Zamira was getting used to Andres going to Dimitri for things —girl-related things.

"Those two are the cutest." Her mama took Dimitri's abandoned seat as she waved a fan in front of her face. "And it's way too hot out there."

"Why do you think I'm in here?" Zamira loved the summer

and outdoor sports but it was June in Florida at noon. She needed a break from the party outside.

"At least the kids will sleep good tonight."

"No kidding."

"So how are things going with you two?" Her mama set her fan down and started making a plate of food, piling on various fruits from one of the platters on the island.

"Great. Amazing, actually. The kids seem to love him so much. I keep waiting for the other shoe to drop." The fact that it hadn't, scared her a little.

"He's a good one. A keeper." Her mama patted her hand once. "You made a good choice with this one."

"I really did," she said.

"So stop waiting for that shoe to drop. You'll run into issues. Of course you will, that's life. But you're not that eighteen-year-old girl anymore. You have a good head on your shoulders now."

"I know." She shifted in her stool and looked out the bank of windows overlooking the gorgeous patio and pool beyond, saw Andres and Dimitri deep in conversation.

And her heart skipped a beat, watching the man she loved with her baby. When he was with them, he was one hundred percent present. And he seemed to love her kids as much as they loved him. He'd been so worried about meeting them, but he'd slid right into their little family seamlessly. Her mom was right, she had to stop being afraid.

This was the next chapter in her life and she was going to embrace it fully. She wasn't going to be afraid to accept that...this was going to work out. She was going to get her happily ever after with a man she'd never seen coming.

EPILOGUE

Five months later

A t the sound of a throat clearing, Dimitri turned, found identical sets of green eyes watching him expectantly. Andres and Elisa.

Zamira and her twins were at his place for the evening and he was cooking for the four of them—though she was currently in his kitchen while these two had snuck up on him. Lately, they'd had a lot of nights—most nights—where it was always the four of them. And he loved it.

"Food's not ready yet," he said, motioning to the three burgers and one black bean burger.

"My black bean burger is definitely done," Elisa said, tossing back her dark, curly hair. "But that's not why we're out here."

Damn, she was right. These things cooked so fast. He slid it onto the plate and turned back to face them. "So what's up? Everything okay?"

"Are you ever going to propose to our mom?" Andres demanded.

He choked on air and dropped his spatula onto the stone with a clatter. "Ah...what?" He cleared his throat. "What I mean is...what?"

Elisa nudged Andres. "You weren't supposed to ask like that," she murmured. "What my brother meant to ask was, well, whatever, are you going to? We've seen the ring," she whispered, and shot a glance over her shoulder.

He followed her gaze. Through the windows, he could see Zamira moving around the kitchen, getting the sides and salads ready. And probably singing to herself. God, he loved her.

He cleared his throat, once, twice. *Damn it.* "I was not aware you had seen the ring."

"Yeah, we saw you practice with it the other day," Andres said.

"Oh my God," his sister growled. Then she sighed long and loud, as she often did with Andres. "We weren't, like, spying on you or anything. We just saw you pop the box open in the kitchen and sort of mime asking her to marry you."

"Then I snuck into your office because I wanted to get a better peek at it," Andres added.

Ever the truthful child.

Elisa covered her face with her hands.

Dimitri held back a laugh at their antics, even as low-grade panic settled in his bones. Okay, forget low-grade. Full-on panic punched through him. He was ready to marry Zamira, loved her more than anything.

Hell, he had the ring in his pocket right now. He always carried it with him, just in case.

But he hadn't been sure it was the right time, hadn't been sure if the kids would want this. And their opinion definitely mattered. He understood that they and Zamira were a package deal. They'd stolen his heart as much as their mom. They were hilarious, a little weird, and such good kids. Good humans. He felt lucky that Zamira had allowed him to be in their lives. And now... "How would you guys feel about me asking her?"

They stared at him in almost shock.

"Uh, we'd love it," Elisa said, as if his question was stupid.

Andres nodded enthusiastically. "Definitely!"

A huge weight that had been bearing down on him suddenly lifted. He sucked in a breath. "Okay. I'll come up with a plan and—"

"Just do it tonight," Andres said.

"I can't do it right now." He needed a plan, order.

"Why not?" Elisa looked back at the already set patio table and the multitude of lights strung up everywhere. "It's perfect."

She and Zamira had added them to his patio a month ago, and he admitted he liked them. There were also lit candles on the table and... "Everything looks really good tonight," he admitted. "Okay, just act normal." He wasn't sure if he was telling them or himself. "Go help your mom set all the sides out." As they ran inside, he grabbed the spare spatula, slid the burgers onto the plate with the black bean one. Looked as if they were a little over-done tonight.

He didn't even care.

Shit.

What if...she said no?

Hell no. He patted his pocket once, even though he knew the ring was there. Energy buzzed through him as everyone strolled outside, started setting the table with the sides.

He put the plate of burgers next to the corn salad and couldn't fight his smile at the way the twins were practically jumping up and down. Yeah, he couldn't wait until after dinner. This was happening now.

"Zamira?"

She turned to look at him, so gorgeous in her dark green dress, her hair down around her face in big, soft curls. And the way she looked at him... It was more than he'd ever hoped for. "Yes?"

He dropped down to one knee, opened the box, his hands actually trembling. "I love you more than I ever thought possible. You've brought me so much joy. *You* are a joy. You and your kids.

I'm hoping you'll agree to marry me, to allow me to be part of your family forever."

Tears streaming down her face, she nodded, a little sob escaping as he slid the ring on her finger. "Yes," she rasped out. "Yes, yes."

The kids started cheering as he pulled her into his arms and then they found themselves being tackled by both of them.

"We're totally moving in here!" Elisa shouted. "More bathroom space and a huge pool!"

Andres just let out a whooping sound, making both of them laugh.

"You sure you know what you're getting into?" Zamira murmured, linking her hands behind his neck as she pressed into him.

"Hell yeah, I do." The biggest adventure of his life.

These were his people. He'd never thought he'd have a family like this, but now that he did he was going to protect and cherish them for the rest of his life.

Dear Readers,

Thank you for reading Deadly Protector! If you'd like to stay in touch and be the first to learn about new releases you can:

- Sign up for my monthly newsletter at: www. katiereus.com
- Follow me on Bookbub: https://www.bookbub.com/ profile/katie-reus
- Find me on Facebook: https://www. facebook.com/katiereusauthor
- Follow me on Instagram: https://www. instagram.com/katiereusauthor/

Also, please consider leaving a review at one of your favorite online retailers. It's a great way to help other readers discover new books and I appreciate all reviews.

Happy reading,

Katie

ACKNOWLEDGMENTS

For Kaylea Cross, you've been here from the start and I'm so grateful to have you as a critique partner and a best friend. As always, I'm grateful to Julia for thorough edits on another Red Stone Security book. I'm so glad you get my sense of humor. Sarah, you're the best, now and always. Jaycee, thank you for (another) cover! I'm also incredibly grateful to my readers, especially my Red Stone Security readers—you guys kept asking for more and I'm so glad you did. It's been wonderful jumping back into this world (it's like a warm visit with old friends). As always, I'm thankful to my family, and especially my mom, who has been helping out the last year in ways I didn't realize I needed. Thank you, thank you!

ABOUT THE AUTHOR

Katie Reus is the *USA Today* bestselling author of the Red Stone Security series, the Ancients Rising series and the Redemption Harbor series. She fell in love with romance at a young age thanks to books she pilfered from her mom's stash. Years later she loves reading romance almost as much as she loves writing it.

However, she didn't always know she wanted to be a writer. After changing majors many times, she finally graduated summa cum laude with a degree in psychology. Not long after that she discovered a new love. Writing. She now spends her days writing paranormal romance and sexy romantic suspense. If you would like to be notified of future releases, please visit her website: https://katiereus.com and join her newsletter.

Complete Booklist

Ancients Rising
Ancient Protector
Ancient Enemy
Ancient Enforcer
Ancient Vendetta
Ancient Retribution
Ancient Vengeance

Darkness Series
Darkness Awakened
Taste of Darkness
Beyond the Darkness
Hunted by Darkness
Into the Darkness
Saved by Darkness
Guardian of Darkness
Sentinel of Darkness
A Very Dragon Christmas
Darkness Rising

Deadly Ops Series
Targeted
Bound to Danger
Chasing Danger
Shattered Duty
Edge of Danger
A Covert Affair

Endgame Trilogy
Bishop's Knight
Bishop's Queen

Bishop's Endgame

MacArthur Family Series
Falling for Irish
Unintended Target
Saving Sienna

Moon Shifter Series
Alpha Instinct
Lover's Instinct
Primal Possession
Mating Instinct
His Untamed Desire
Avenger's Heat
Hunter Reborn
Protective Instinct
Dark Protector
A Mate for Christmas

O'Connor Family Series
Merry Christmas, Baby
Tease Me, Baby
It's Me Again, Baby
Mistletoe Me, Baby

Red Stone Security Series®
No One to Trust
Danger Next Door
Fatal Deception
Miami, Mistletoe & Murder
His to Protect
Breaking Her Rules
Protecting His Witness
Sinful Seduction

Under His Protection
Deadly Fallout
Sworn to Protect
Secret Obsession
Love Thy Enemy
Dangerous Protector
Lethal Game
Secret Enemy
Saving Danger
Guarding Her
Deadly Protector
Danger Rising

Redemption Harbor Series®
Resurrection
Savage Rising
Dangerous Witness
Innocent Target
Hunting Danger
Covert Games
Chasing Vengeance

Sin City Series (the Serafina)
First Surrender
Sensual Surrender
Sweetest Surrender
Dangerous Surrender
Deadly Surrender

Verona Bay Series
Dark Memento
Deadly Past
Silent Protector

Linked books

Retribution

Tempting Danger

Non-series Romantic Suspense

Running From the Past

Dangerous Secrets

Killer Secrets

Deadly Obsession

Danger in Paradise

His Secret Past

Paranormal Romance

Destined Mate

Protector's Mate

A Jaguar's Kiss

Tempting the Jaguar

Enemy Mine

Heart of the Jaguar

Made in the USA
Columbia, SC
11 July 2022

63204054R00107